The Cost of Living

by M.L. Pressman

ISBN eBook:	ISBN-10:	0988572028
	ISBN-13:	978-0-9885720-2-7
ISBN Hardcover:	ISBN-10:	0988572001
	ISBN-13:	978-0-9885720-0-3
ISBN Paperback:	ISBN-10:	098857201X
	ISBN-13:	978-0-9885720-1-0

DEDICATION

This book is dedicated to my fantastic family, they make me smile with simple memories. K, J and O, I love you so very much...

Sue, for living some of these with me...

Many thanks need to be expressed to the numerous people who provided the encouragement I needed for finishing and publishing this book, especially:

Maddy and Alex (always inspiration to entertain), Aunt Pearl and Meridith for the extra push, Beth Kallman Warner for the edit and the guidance, and G.C. for his ability to work with me through all the (fun-loving) abuse.

...and to the real Jean Kurchowski. What a mess you created, but I'm trying to be better.

TABLE OF CONTENTS

— Chapter One —

THE COST OF A MOVIE

The first time I realized my mother was crazy, I think I was eight. I must have been eight because it was shortly after she and I moved into our house in 1974, the same house that she occupied until the day she died. In between those two milestones, my mother let a perfectly solid, split-level house on half an acre of land in Huntington, Long Island, become the laughing stock of the street.

On the outside the paint was chipping, the fence was falling, the grass was dead, the bushes were overgrown, the leaves were never raked, and the gutters were never cleared. Whatever junk she couldn't stuff into the garage could be found lodged against the frame of the house. The interior walls were decorated with either paneling or flat green paint. The carpeting was a dirty brown, mostly because from the day we moved in, she never replaced it. But the house was only one of the reasons why my mother was the "crazy lady" on the block. Every street in every neighborhood of every town in every state has one. On mine, there was my mom, Jean Kurchowski.

Jean Kurchowski was single, raising me on her own. When I realized that all the other kids in our neighborhood had daddies, I questioned what had happened to mine. My mother told me that my father was declared legally stupid by New York State and therefore was incapable of helping to raise a family. She went on to say that Lester Hargrove, my father, had been ordered by the courts to work go-nowhere jobs, remain emotionally void, and contract sexually transmitted diseases until he was dead. She summed it up by reminding me that I had better do well in school or else the State would declare me legally stupid as well.

Like me, Jean was also an only child. The only other relative I had contact with during my formative years was my grandmother, who lived in a senior's community in Coconut Creek, FL, near Boca Raton. Inasmuch, growing up, I was naturally curious about the rest of my family and all the minor details. I remember once asking Jean what her middle name was. She told me she didn't have one. I found that strange, since I had a middle name. Jean had bestowed upon me the full title Caroline Cecilia Kurchowski. I've always loved the first two-thirds of that name.

My mother said she didn't have a middle name because "we were so poor, my parents couldn't afford one." As a six-year old, you tend to believe the bizarre things your parents tell you. For several years, I grew up believing that my mother was deprived of a second name because the name store had raised their prices. By the time I was a teenager, I realized if there was any plausibility to this being true, it wasn't due to any lack of wealth, but that Jean was just unwilling to part with her money.

To put it bluntly, my mother was cheap. Just like her mother, and if there's any validity to the gene pool, her mother before her. "Cost" was a persistent topic of conversation for Jean; she was obsessed with prices. There was nothing in my mother's house that hadn't been purchased without a coupon, on sale, or at a garage sale. Jean often said she was this way because she came from Depression-era parents. Another popular tale was that both her parents had come down with pneumonia at the same time and were confined to their beds for eight months, during which they lost the family business - forcing her to run the household at the tender age of twelve. My mother had quite an imagination.

I later discovered that my grandfather had been a moderately successful insurance agent and the family had lived comfortably in Hempstead, Long Island. They'd had no trouble making ends meet, vacationed often, and paid for my mother's college education with nary a dent to their bank account.

Following college, my mother had gone to work as an accountant. She was never forthcoming about how she met my father, other than to say, "In the usual way." Details were not provided, but to her detriment, her version of the "dead-beat womanizer whose skin is deteriorating from his many venereal diseases" left an image of my mother as a barfly who made for easy pickings. Her Reader's Digest version is that she met my father, got pregnant, and then, when he opted not to return home one day, she went back to work at a large accounting firm.

My mother's income wouldn't categorize us as Upper Middle Class, but I knew we weren't poor. We moved into a good neighborhood and ate well. Even though (under the guise of being poor) she would refuse to spend ten dollars on a new toy for me, she would gladly fork over an equal amount on ten one-dollar toys from the yard sale down the street. It was all about quantity, not quality. In other words, Jean was just cheap.

It would be unfair to only characterize my mother in this way. She was also a first-class fibber. She was quite a storyteller when it came to denying events in her life or the way she chose to live. Inevitably and unfortunately, I would uncover the truth; the hard, painful truth that would make me look at my mother and think, "Who the hell are you?" Sometimes the lies turned out to be mundane and laughable, but there were others that triggered traumatic events in my life. Hence, the stories that follow…

The first time I can remember Jean and I fighting was the first time I thought she was crazy. One Sunday she decided to take me to a movie. It was a matinee, which was only half price. She tried to pass me off as a two-year old to get me in for free, but the ticket seller didn't buy it. Neither did the manager. The only one doing the buying was my mother, at full price. Due to her stubborn, innate desire to haggle, we missed the first ten minutes of "Ghostbusters."

Finally we entered the theatre, which was filled with parents and their raucous kids, forcing us to take a pair of seats near the back. About halfway through the movie, Jean leaned over and whispered, "Would you like some popcorn?" This was a deceivingly defining moment in my life. Popcorn? Everyone knows they overcharge for popcorn! Knowing the odds of my mother buying something at the concession stand were higher than the sun in the sky, I hadn't even thought about asking. I looked up at her with what I thought had to be a twinkle in my eye. This was a moment I was going to cherish forever. I nodded enthusiastically.

Jean rose from her seat and began pacing up and down the aisle. Immediately, I sensed that something bad was about to happen. She paced with purpose. She paced like she had a plan. As I would discover through the years, she always had a plan, and her plans were always devious. Oh, not in some twisted, sociopathic, Jean ends up in jail and I end up in a foster home kind of way. Her plans were just devious enough, just ethically questionable enough to make me feel as if I wanted to nail wooden planks to our doors and windows and never be seen by public eyes again. The way Jean was pacing in that theater, her head nodding as the plan was coming together nicely, I knew that this was going to be monumental in making me feel miniscule.

She began to take on the presence of a maniacal clown, smiling with widened eyes, her head bobbing as she zeroed in on her prey. It was all unfolding in slow motion to me. I was clearly being punished for something I must have done, because this was the moment God decided to freeze me in time.

I slumped into my seat. Toward the middle of the theatre, Jean leaned over and asked another mother, "Are you done with that?" Bewildered, the woman handed my mother an emptied popcorn bag. Jean tore a hole in the bottom of the bag. She marched back up the aisle, grabbed my arm, and said, "Let's go."

The Cost of Living

"Can I help you?" the teenage boy inquired innocently from behind the concession counter. His voice cracked and his futile attempts to catch himself caused him to spit on the counter, the snacks and us. He also had bad acne. This wouldn't matter at all, except he had a nasty habit of pinching the pimples on his face when he was nervous.

Jean made him very nervous. I suddenly couldn't help but wonder who the genius was that, in their managerial wisdom, chose this pustule-popper to sell food. I couldn't help feeling a tad nauseous. However, my queasiness was mostly brought on by Jean's attack on this poor fool, who was soon to learn a lesson from a formidable opponent – a lesson that even a Harvard economics professor couldn't teach.

"I just bought this popcorn, and there's a hole in the bottom." To further her case, Jean presented the boy with "Exhibit A" – the fraudulently torn popcorn bag.

"My daughter got so upset, she spilled the whole bag on the floor."

"I'm sorry, Maam. I'll get you another one right away."

"You ought to throw in a soda, for making her cry."

"Absolutely, Maam."

As the nervous young man turned his back to retrieve our snacks, my mother looked down at me and winked.

I became frightened. Being seven, I still had a hard time discerning what was unethical bordering on illegal. I was still in the stage where a child believes that their parent could never, would never, ever, ever be naughty. Jean was my safe haven. She was the angel sent from the heavens to watch over me. Angels don't lie for free popcorn! It isn't supposed to work like that.

Yet, even though I couldn't put my finger on it at the time, something didn't feel right about what had transpired. All I could do was say thank you to the nice man like my mother told me to, and return to the movie.

The rest of the film was quite discomforting for me. I fidgeted in my seat, but I was unsure as to why I was so jittery. One thing I knew, I didn't want to be in that theatre anymore. I prayed for the end credits to appear so we could go home. Finally it was over, and as the lights went up I made a beeline for the exit. I was almost out the door when my mother tugged on my shirt.

"Isn't there another movie playing upstairs?"

"Mom, I just want to go home. Please."

"Nonsense. For these prices they should show a double feature."

"Please, Mom!" I pleaded. I was on the verge of sobbing.

"Hurry. No one's looking," she whispered deviously. And she dragged me to see "Gremlins." They frightened me.

The Cost of Living

The entire ride home I was quiet. She had angered me in some way. I could sense some kind of betrayal, some dishonesty between us. I mean, the conniving for popcorn and soda was bad enough, but now we had actually stolen a whole movie. All through the second feature I'd felt as though the gremlins themselves were staring at us, provoking us to get up and admit our guilt.

"What's with you, pouty-puss?"

I wouldn't answer her. She pulled the car over.

"Is this how you're going to be the rest of the day?" she asked.

"How come you made me do that?"

"Do what?" As if she was unaware of the heinous act she'd committed.

"Make me go to that movie. You didn't pay for it."

I thought she'd be proud of my integrity; the virtue of a child in the prime of her character-building years, looking to her mother to set the ethical bar. I needed a mother who would own up to any wrongdoing. Jean was not this mother.

"Caroline, when you're an adult you'll understand that sometimes people charge too much for things. For what we paid to go in there, we should have gotten three movies, four bags of popcorn, two sodas, licorice and ice cream. That's what it was worth. Trust me."

But I didn't trust her. I knew she was wrong, and it was painful to know. When we got home, I stomped into my room and slammed the door. I laid down on my bed, sulking. Dusk quickly approached and the room turned dark, but I didn't get up to switch on the light. I allowed the moon to slightly illuminate my room. I was so angry with Jean that I wanted to show her I could be brave, that I didn't need her.

Just as my eyelids grew heavy and I was about to drift asleep, my bedroom door creaked open. I could see Jean's silhouette formed by the hallway light.

"Caroline, I have something for you."

Children should never fall for this ploy. However, a child has little patience to hold onto their emotions when the prospect of owning a new toy or enjoying a butter crunch ice cream cone is dangled in front of their face.

"What is it?" I asked, trying not to sound too eager, but curiously annoyed.

She turned on the light and I squinted from the sudden attack on my eyes. From behind her back she produced a book and a pen.

"This is a journal. Whenever you get angry with me again, I want you to write down everything that happened and everything you feel. Get it out of your system and then we can be pals again! Okay?" I nodded and accepted the book. My eyelids were dropping and I was too exhausted to stay mad.

Of course, that didn't keep me from being disappointed. I was hoping for a Barbie doll, but I thanked her anyway. The journal was covered with a stitched, flowered pattern of violet and pink. A blue ribbon bookmark was attached to the binding. I flipped through the blank pages that would eventually feature my hopes, dreams, fears, aspirations, loves, and losses... except not all the pages were blank.

The first eight pages had doodles in them with a few badly misspelled sentences, such as, "I fed my fish today" and "Today I threw up green." On the inside of the back cover, scribbled in pencil, was the name "Fran McCricket." The journal was second-hand. Apparently, after throwing up green, Fran never wrote in the book again, and I didn't think I would either.

As Jean walked out of the room, she paused for a moment before switching the light off. "Remember, it's only you and me, kiddo."

I did write in that journal. Those times when I was alone and I felt nobody could truly understand the pain, those times when I felt ashamed to be who I was, those times when I wanted to run away and change my name so nobody could find me. Those were the times that I would write in my journal. They were pretty much all the times I was in a pivotal rift with my mother, Jean Kurchowski.

Now, with Jean gone, I've decided to abridge my journal into one cohesive story. I've shaped several excerpts from each year into chapters. In this way I could reflect on our relationship and come to understand and appreciate Jean Kurchowski even more. Now when I want to remember the beauty of her lunacy, I can take a quick glimpse into my life with "The Crazy Lady of Linden Drive."

— Chapter Two —
THE COST OF
LIVING NEXT DOOR

My first year in our new neighborhood was a tough adjustment. Our house was situated on a corner and our backyard was the only thing separating us from a sump, a giant fenced hole the town dug as a reservoir for excess water. Never had I seen even a puddle collect in that hole. It was just a big crater behind the house.

The only home that connected our property to the rest of the neighborhood belonged to the Caldwells, a family that wasn't particularly friendly. In fact, we rarely saw them.

The very first day we moved in, Naomi Caldwell, a beauty-salon queen in a beige pantsuit adorned with rhinestones, greeted us by saying, "Thank God you're white."

A statement like that did not sit well with Jean, and in her head a war had been declared.

In addition to Naomi, the Caldwell family included her husband Al and their three children - Maggie, Jill, and Damen. The middle child, Jill, was my age. I watched by my window hoping to catch her playing outside, so I could conveniently be in the next yard and possibly strike up a friendship. However, Maggie and Jill were neither seen nor heard from other than those fleeting moments when they were getting in and out of the family car, a metallic green Cadillac.

The boy, Damen, was always outside, but he was also always alone. He would throw a football to himself or hit a whiffleball into the air and chase it down. He seemed to resemble an eager mutt trying to get the attention of his owner.

Damen tended to "broadcast" his actions, as if he were playing sports on television. It was almost cute. I wondered why he didn't have any friends to join him. Finally, I gave up on the girls and decided to play with Damen, who was bigger than me even though he was a year younger.

Nervously, I approached him.

"What do you want?" he asked. He was holding the whiffleball bat like a caveman holding a club.

"I thought you might want somebody to play with. I can pitch." I could, too. I had a little bit of tomboy in me. Though I was no spectacular athlete, I had a certain amount of prowess here and there.

"Girls can't pitch, stupid." I immediately sensed why Damen had nobody to play with.

"Why don't you let me try? Or maybe you're afraid." This was a dare, and Damen was apparently well on his way to one day being an abusive husband who did not take kindly to women getting the better of him.

"I'll give you one chance to get it over the plate," he said.

He handed me the ball and I backed up about fifteen feet. I tried to ease the tension by incorporating some unusually goofy arm twirls and leg kicks into my wind-up, but Damen had no sense of humor and no patience. "Just pitch the ball already, dammit!"

I turned serious and whipped the ball toward him. Now anyone who's played whiffleball knows that the plastic configuration of the ball can cause wild movement in the pitch, depending on how you hold it and twist your wrist. I did not know this at the time. However, I must have done something right, because the ball spun toward Damen's bat and at the last second dipped down, then nearly straight up. Damen took a healthy swing, but he didn't hit the ball; he hit the ground with his butt as his body twisted completely around.

"Wow," I said, impressed with my own ability. Then I laughed.

Embarrassed, Damen stood up and came towards me with the bat.

"What's so funny?" He held the bat high, as if it was going to come crashing down on me. Then he chased me around the yard, swinging at my head. I didn't know if he was missing on purpose, but I was scared and began screaming. Jean must have heard my cries because she stormed out the front door and grabbed the bat out of Damen's hands.

"What's going on here?"

Damen pointed at me. "She's stupid."

"She is, is she? So you decided to hit her with a bat? Well, let's see how that works on you since I think you're stupid." She smacked him on his butt with the bat, not too hard, but enough to make a point. Damen yelped and ran toward his house. Jean chased after him, every now and then putting the bat to his behind, and not letting him near the sanctuary of his home.

I glanced over at the Caldwell's porch and caught Maggie and Jill watching this spectacle from just inside the door. Their faces were void of expression and they didn't blink. They were like robots, uncaring of their brother's dilemma. Perhaps they hated him as well.

As my mother chased Damen around the yard, apparently enjoying the fracas, a group of kids stopped their bicycles to watch. I walked over to them, hoping to get lost in the crowd.

"That lady's nuts," one of them observed. I nodded to myself in agreement.

One of the girls, a quiet type who was slightly chubby and wearing glasses, asked me, "That's your mom, isn't it?"

I didn't answer.

Suddenly, all the children were looking at me. The chubby girl asked again. "Isn't that your mom?"

"I guess."

All attention turned back to Jean chasing this little dervish of a boy in circles. Damen was screaming and it was hard to discern whether he was having fun or fleeing for his life.

Just then, the Caldwell's front door swung open violently, slamming against the house. Naomi Caldwell stood on the porch and yelled to my mother. "Are you insane!?"

Jean stopped dead in her tracks. Damen rushed to his mother's side and strapped himself to her leg.

"You tell your kid not to hit girls, or else we're going to hit back," Jean said.

Naomi stepped closer to my mother, dragging Damen with her.

"Don't tell me how to raise my kids."

"Seems to me you don't raise them at all."

"How dare you! Who do you think you are?"

"Whoever I am, I guess you should have wished I was black. Come home now, C.C." My mother started towards our

17

house. I looked over toward the chubby girl, pleading with my eyes to include me in something so I didn't have to join my mother.

"I'm Beth," the girl said.

I yelled to Jean, "Mom, can I play with Beth?"

My mother stopped short of the porch and narrowed her eyes in Beth's direction, as if she were scrutinizing her character. "When you can't see your hand in front of your face, you come back inside, got it?"

"Got it!" I turned to Beth. "Okay?"

"I guess." She slid up on her bicycle seat so I could fit behind her. As I straddled the bike, Beth asked, "Is your mother always crazy like that?"

I replied simply, "Yes."

— Chapter Three —

THE COST OF
MAKING FRIENDS

Though Beth Voorhees and I instantly became the best of friends, a full year passed before I would let her inside my house. When we got together to worship Scott Baio and write love letters to Rick Springfield, it was always done in her bedroom.

I was embarrassed, to say the least, at how my mother kept our home. I attempted several times to tidy a room or throw some things away (thinking she wouldn't notice), but I was constantly admonished by her to leave everything in the chaotic ruins that cluttered every square inch.

In no exaggerated terms, Jean had the cleaning sense of a bedraggled junkman. The house had three bedrooms; hers, mine and a guestroom. The guestroom was littered with boxes upon boxes of purchases that Jean had deemed "deals." Each box was designated in black magic marker by the contents. There was the "Christmas" box, which contained everything from tree decorations to gift ideas. There was the "Birthday" box, which seemed to be filled mostly with presents for me. Then there was the "Kitchen" box, full of knickknacks to make cooking easier. The boxes were stacked on top of one another in no particular order, and it made entering the room an impossibility.

The most obvious problem with Jean's system was that she never actually used any of the products she collected. I never received what was in the boxes marked for my benefit. She just kept adding to the boxes and then adding more boxes.

The most unsightly part of the house was the insides of the refrigerators. We owned not just one refrigerator, but three. Every time Jean went grocery shopping, she was sure to bring home a ridiculous amount of groceries to feed two people. If she saw something on sale, she bought it. It did not matter in the least whether either of us enjoyed "Frozen Spaghetti in Clam Sauce." If it was half-price, she grabbed double the amount. Of course, it never occurred to her that even if we ate only half of what she bought, she was still spending the same money - thereby never saving a cent. At least 75 percent of her purchases remained untouched, hence the money was completely wasted. Jean's economics were all about supply. She never took time or had interest to consider demand.

The main refrigerator, the one that held food for immediate consumption, could be found in the kitchen. However, it wasn't necessarily filled with food that would be immediately consumed. Instead, plastic Tupperware containers packed with leftovers were jammed as far back in the racks as could possibly fit. Tiny packages of ketchup, mustard, mayonnaise, soy sauce, hot mustard, orange duck sauce, relish, horseradish and any other condiment from a fast food take-out restaurant could turn up in, on, beside or underneath anything. Spilled juices from unknown sources stuck to the door and shelves, creating an adhesive that forced you to retrieve each item with a hearty tug.

The second refrigerator was located in the basement. This one held junk food and beverages. Aside from cases of generic sodas there were Twinkies, Chocodiles, Bagel-Dogs (hot dogs wrapped in bagel-like bread), Ring Dings, Ho-Hos, and at least twenty Entenmann's cakes from the bakery outlet which sold unsold desserts at low-low prices. Stale cakes at a fresh price.

The outside refrigerator was actually a freezer. It was stored in the garage and every space of it was occupied by some kind of meat. There were steaks and chopped beef along with packages of whole chickens, chicken legs, chicken breasts, chicken nuggets, chicken strips, chicken wings, and chicken thighs. There were pork chops and lamb chops. There were franks and sausages. All this meat was wedged in every which way, but rarely eaten. Jean Kurchowski was ready to feed every last survivor after Armageddon.

By the time I allowed Beth to witness the warehouse that I called "home," I'd decided that I could not let Jean's habits be a reflection of me. Beth had started to wonder why I never invited her over. Because of her weight and glasses, she was low on self-esteem.

I found out in the course of our first year as friends that Beth had been born in Greece and then adopted by her parents, Flo and Stan. After taking Beth into their home, Flo became pregnant twice and had two boys, leaving Beth always feeling somewhat neglected. It didn't help that she had a much darker, ethnic complexion than the rest of her family, which only added to her feelings of being an outcast. So, in order to make my best friend feel better, I invited her into my home.

I surmised that getting Beth out of the house before Jean returned from work at six would reduce any anxiety by fifty percent. I hoped that Beth wouldn't want to roam the house - that she would be content to play in my room. However, this was not to be. Beth was instantly awed by how much stuff could be in one house. She wandered around carefully, as if she were in a museum.

"There's so much…"

"It's not mine. It's my mother's. You should see the basement and the garage." This was the wrong thing to say, since that was exactly what Beth wanted to do next.

The basement was modest. It was paneled, as many rooms were in those days, and it stored a lot of broken furniture and games. Jean would come home in the station wagon on weekends with any number of items lodged in the back or tied to the roof. More often than not it was some piece of junk that somebody was giving away and she swore she was going to repair it. I never knew if her intention was to eventually sell these items or use them herself, but it didn't matter. Invariably they would sit in the basement, never to be touched again.

There was a couch with ripped upholstery, a chair with the back detached, an air hockey game sans fan, a pogo stick that lost it's go… the list went on and on.

It was to my benefit that Beth had a sense of humor. "You know what you can get from all this stuff?"

"No, what?"

"Cobwebs." This made me laugh.

We began to rummage through the stuff, making fun of each piece. It was like an old Three Stooges movie as we sat on the backless chair and pretended to fall. Beth helped me to relax that day and not feel so inhibited by my mother. Unfortunately, because we were having so much fun, I lost track of the time. I tensed up when I heard the door open and my mother's annoyingly cheerful cry of "Helloooo!" ring throughout the house.

I wanted to tell Beth to be quiet, to hide from my mother, but we had left the basement door open and Jean came down the stairs.

"What are you doing down here?" she asked.

"Nothing, just playing."

"Be careful with this stuff. I'm getting ready to work on it this weekend... You must be Beth. I'm Caroline's mom."

Beth politely held out her hand, "Pleased to meet you, Mrs. Kurchowski. We didn't break anything."

"Everything's already broken," I said.

Jean corrected me, "Nothing's broken. It just needs some TLC. Beth, would you like to stay for dinner?"

Oh my God! Not dinner! Sirens went off in my head. An image of me blocking the refrigerator popped into my head. I wanted to ward off all evil that could be released from the hell of that appliance.

"I'd have to call my mom first."

The Cost of Living

"Come on upstairs, but hurry. I brought home pizza. We have to eat before it gets cold."

Pizza! Yes! I breathed a sigh of relief. Beth received permission from her mother and the three of us sat down to pepperoni pizza. My mother would get up every now and then to futz about the kitchen, pretending to be like Carol Brady. I thought how odd it was that Jean could seem so perfectly normal around other people when she tried, but when she let her guard down, the "crazy lady" would appear. Then, before I could do anything, her mask was about to come off.

Beth and I were acting like typical ten-year old girls, playing with our food and giggling about boys in school, when it happened. Just above Beth's head, a crack appeared in the ceiling. I told Beth to look, but she thought I was trying to fool her.

"I'm serious, look up."

"I'm not falling for that."

Suddenly, like a piece from a jigsaw puzzle, a small part of the ceiling fell off and missed Beth's head by no more than a hair's breadth. I couldn't take my eyes off the hole when a tiny, hairy butt fell into it. It was a mouse and it was stuck. It wriggled and wriggled trying to right itself when a leg busted through, and I shrieked. I must have scared it because when

Beth finally believed that I saw something, she looked skyward and the mouse peed on her. Beth became hysterical and ran around the kitchen, not wanting to touch anything. She was hoping that someone would hand her a wet rag, but I was too mesmerized by the mouse.

Jean finally realized that my scream was not a child's playful screech and came over to see what the commotion was about. Beth, with her eyes closed, ran into her. Jean pushed her aside when she noticed the squirming mouse in the hole in the ceiling.

"Everybody quiet!"

I shut my mouth, and Beth, her body shaking, calmed to a whimper. Jean took a pen and stood on Beth's chair. She put pen to mouse butt and heaved him into the hole. We heard the little rodent scamper across the ceiling. We followed him with our eyes into the foyer. Jean nonchalantly stepped off the chair and said, "Who wants some dessert?"

Beth didn't. She just wanted to go home. Jean drove her down the street and Beth ran into her house. When we returned to our driveway, Jean sensed my aggravation.

"Honey, you can't be mad at me. It's not my fault there's a mouse in the house. They need to find places to live, too."

"Maybe if the house wasn't so dirty…"

"C.C., I work all day, I only have so much time on the weekends."

I told her, "I could clean."

"You can vacuum and do dishes. That's good enough. Don't worry. One of these days I'll get organized."

This would turn out to be a hollow promise that I would hear every time the subject was broached. I knew deep down inside that "organization" to Jean meant rearranging her boxes in some nonsensical order and pulling everything out of the refrigerator to wipe down the shelves, only to stuff it all back inside.

It took several months before Beth would visit again. The mouse incident had completely freaked her out. Eventually she got used to Jean's slovenly habits, as did I. I had to. I had no choice. Every now and then, I would get on my mother's case about throwing things out and making the place neater, but it fell on deaf ears. This was who she was and it was her house.

That night, with fireflies lighting up the backyard sky, my mother and I sat on the back porch bench in the heavy, humid summer air. We laughed at each other as we painted our faces with ice cream. My mother took a breath and looked to the stars. I watched her and realized that she'd really had a good time that day, and at the end of the day she needed someone to share it with. I was no longer her co-conspirator. I was her "listener," the person she needed to tell good things to, because she had no one else.

At that moment all was forgotten, and I was happy to be that person for her.

— Chapter Four —

THE COST OF
SHOPPING FOR SALES

"Just get in the car, Caroline."

"No!"

Yes, I was being stubborn, but I felt I had a good case. It was a beautiful, sun drenched summer day, and I did not want to waste it. I had plans with Beth to go to the school playground and shoot off some fireworks that she had lifted from her older brother's dresser. The playground was usually vacant during summer vacation, so we figured we could exact some kind of vengeance on the school without being caught.

Beth and I had become close friends. We talked so much during class, plotting and scheming numerous fantastical scenarios, that we often had to be separated. Our teacher had already labeled us troublemakers and it seemed as though we had an obligation to ourselves to live up to the name.

Unfortunately, on this particular day, Jean wanted to take me on one of her bargain-hunts. My mother was a compulsive shopper. It was not for survival and it was not her hobby; it was her soul. She could spend the better part of a lifetime in and out of department malls, gift shops and discount stores, even places that sold used underwear, as long as the front window was plastered with "Sale" signs all over it. Jean Kurchowski would drive a hundred miles and waste tens of dollars in gas if she could save a quarter.

It seemed to me that Jean's perspective on life worked two ways: Firstly, life was a race and the person with the most stuff in the end wins; secondly, paying less than what another store charges puts you in the lead. Thus, her primary objective was to get the most stuff for the least amount of money. This sounds perfectly reasonable in theory, but Jean bought anything and everything. She wasn't a pack rat; she was a pack elephant.

Spending the day rushing from mall to mall and store to store is not an eleven-year old's idea of fun. It couldn't even be considered quality time, since Jean and I never talked on these outings. I would stare out the window brooding while Jean's eyes darted about the road, seeking her next prey. She interpreted my lack of enthusiasm as being spoiled, and claimed she was compensating my time by buying me clothes. However, these garments she made me wear were always in bad taste. If I told her I didn't like a particular shirt or pair of pants, she would buy them anyway, telling me, "Put it in your closet, you might like it later." A year later, this philosophy invariably led to the following exchange:

"Mom, I need new clothes."

"You have plenty of clothes in your closet that you haven't even worn yet."

"I don't like those clothes. I never liked those clothes."

"Then why did you have me buy them for you?"

I had decided I wasn't going to do this anymore and struggled whenever she wanted me to get in the car. I felt like the dog that knew it was doomed to go to the veterinarian for a shot. I howled and pulled away, but to no avail.

This particular day turned out to be the worst. Jean always had her designated targets, which she hit without fail. Most of them were clearance centers and bargain basement stores that were filled with battling women. Jean neglected to realize that for the most part, the prices were slashed because the merchandise was unsightly and nobody wanted it. They were often defective products that Jean deemed "good enough for the price."

One of these stores, Flora & Bailer, was in the midst of a "blowout" sale. Blowout sale usually meant a blow-up between Jean and me; and this day turned out to be no exception. Dragging me by the arm, Jean shoved her way through every department, every aisle, and every rack. It was a free-for-all, and Jean loved all things free. She was in her element. She had a wild look in her eye and pure instinct took over.

I decided to try to maintain my patience until it was over. I figured if didn't complain, I might be able to finagle an ice cream out of the deal.

Then, the unthinkable happened. Jean overheard a fellow obsessive shopper conversing with the manager, who was telling this woman that a new store had just opened in Morristown, New Jersey, and the store we were in was being turned into the ultimate discount outlet. I thought to myself, "Good Lord, she's going to drag me here until I drop dead."

What I didn't anticipate was an enterprising idea entering Jean's perverse head. She sprang to life, racing from bin to bin, looking for each and every price tag she could find that listed the original price along with a sale price sticker.

After two hours she'd purchased fourteen shirts, twenty-three pants, eight sets of shoes and a man's suit. Totaled, her purchases came to $1,172 and change. As the cashier swiped her credit card, Jean anxiously rocked in place and muttered to herself, "Come on. Go through." She was praying she hadn't over-extended her credit. When she heard the beep accepting her purchases, I thought I heard a barely audible "Yippee" escape her lips.

To get from Huntington, Long Island to Morristown, New Jersey, a person must drive across five highways and over two toll bridges. The round-trip exacts one hundred and sixteen miles off the car and over a half a tank of gas. Yet, this was where we were heading when Jean came up with the idea to sell back the discounted clothes to Flora & Bailer through the new store in New Jersey at the original prices.

As we drove along the Long Island Expressway, I caught glimpses of children racing around backyards, cannon-balling into pools, and screeching as they jumped through sprinklers. I was envious of their situations and resentful of mine. Then, as I looked in the back of the station wagon at the pile of gaudy clothes, a thought occurred to me, one I should have kept to myself. However, I made the drastic mistake of thinking out loud.

"Won't they be suspicious that you're returning so much?"

After some intense scrutiny, Jean pulled off the highway before reaching the Throgs Neck Bridge and drove back toward the original Flora & Bailer. After sitting in traffic for a while we finally arrived at the store, where Jean left me in the car and promptly returned most of the clothes. She hopped back in and sped off like a bandit, which is in fact what she was.

By the time we got to Morristown it was late afternoon. I was tired, hungry, sweaty and cranky; but Jean was on a mission and pretty much tuned out my complaints. We walked into the store and headed straight for the returns. Jean didn't even look down at me as she said through the corner of her mouth, "Let me do the talking."

Let her do the talking? What did she think I was doing there? Did she think I was in cahoots with her? Go ahead, do the talking, you loon. Leave me out of your schemes. Just get me home and feed me, please!

Jean placed the remaining items on the return counter. She had peeled the sales labels off the tags so that only the original prices appeared.

"Hi, somebody bought these for me and my family, as a gift, so I don't have the receipts," she explained to the employee of Flora & Bailer.

The woman working the counter - a disinterested twenty-year old, sneered at the garments since she knew that returns unaccompanied by receipts meant extra work for her. As the clerk sorted through the shirts and pants and the suit, Jean, her eyes wide open, intently followed the woman's hands from tag to tag.

"Wait, I think you missed one," Jean pointed out.

The Cost of Living

The woman looked up at her and sighed. She started all over again.

I hid between my mother and the counter. I couldn't believe she was pulling a fast one and had the nerve to push her luck like that. In a way, I wanted to admire her nerve, but I was too petrified that we were going to jail.

After what seemed like an eternity, my mother received a refund on her credit card for a total profit of $33.94.

When we finally parked the station wagon in the driveway at home, I noticed the lights on in our neighbors' kitchens. I imagined families sitting at dinner tables, the children still excited from their active summer day. I could practically hear the spinning of tall tales involving home runs that were hit, giant trees that were climbed, and races that were won. I thought about how the mommies and daddies would barely be able to get their kids to bed; the children giddy with the notion of another perfect day of summer fun that awaited them tomorrow.

I, on the other hand, had done nothing and yet I was exhausted.

Lying on my bed, I calculated what it must have cost my mother to earn $33.94. There was no doubt in my mind that after tolls and gas, that little sum would dwindle by at least half.

I didn't even add up depreciation to the station wagon, which was on its last legs, or time spent, which, to me, was priceless.

When I went downstairs for dinner, I found leftover meatloaf steaming on my plate. Leaning on one arm, I cheerlessly picked at my food. My mother on the other hand, talked incessantly. Jean was still on her shopping high, like the neighborhood children who had played all day. The stores were her playground, and though it wasn't much, she had won at the end of the day. She had hit her home-run.

"We had such fun today, didn't we, C.C.?" When she called me C.C., it meant we were friends. She only called me Caroline when she was being a mother.

"Uh-huh." Though I was mad at her, I didn't really want to spoil her day by getting into a fight.

"We should do that more often. Just the girls, right?"

"Maybe not too soon." She glanced my way and finally spotted the frown on my face. She gave me a smile.

"You know what girls do at the end of a girl's day together?" She went to the freezer and dug through frozen packages of chicken, meat, spaghetti sauce, and tupperware containers full of leftovers she'd been saving for a couple of years. Finally, she pulled out and presented me with a tub full of Rocky Road Ice Cream, my favorite flavor.

— Chapter Five —

THE COST OF
A DAY IN THE PARK

Jean held out the flier, which read in a bold font, "All Parents and Children are Welcome." The date was a Saturday at a roller rink that transformed into a massive Flea Market on Sundays. It was at the Flea Market where Jean noticed the flier posted on the entrance door. The occasion was a picnic for "Parents Without Partners," to be held on the following Saturday in Hecksher Park, about two miles from our house. The notice boasted an assortment of activities such as softball, frisbee football, races and barbecues.

"Sounds like fun, doesn't it?" Jean asked.

"I won't know anybody there."

"That's the point, silly. We'll meet new people, people who are in the same situation we are."

"What situation is that?"

"Well, your situation is a child with only one parent, and mine is a parent without a partner."

This seemed to be a good time for me to inquire once again, "And where is my father, anyway…?"

"I told you, he got sent away for being stupid."

"Mom…" My voice was pleading with her to tell me the truth.

"C.C., I honestly don't know where your father is. I'm sure he's with all the other stupid people. Now do you want to go to this picnic or not?"

"No. I don't need any more new friends."

She kneeled down and peered into my eyes. With the utmost sincerity, she quietly said with a tinge of loneliness, "Caroline, I need new friends."

For the next week I prayed for rain on Saturday, although I knew that would only provide a short stay of execution. My mother scoured garage sales for athletic equipment, to give her a way to break the ice. She acquired a baseball glove that was for a left-handed person, a catcher's chest protector that stunk from mold, one cracked shin guard, and a lacrosse stick with netting that was ripped down the center. I wasn't sure exactly what my mother intended to do with the stuff, but she was determined to look prepared.

The Cost of Living

The following Saturday, with the June sun shining on colorful flora in the park, Jean and I arrived and unloaded the station wagon. Aside from the sporting gear we brought a cooler filled with the best ground beef and hot dogs Jean could dig out of the freezer. I was frightened to look at the dates on the packaging. I could only assume I was older than the food, but not by much.

Jean didn't hesitate to jump into the fray. She had dressed up in a Spring ensemble that accentuated her best features. Her loose-fitting shirt, yellow with a pattern of pink lilies, discreetly covered her cellulite. The day before, Jean had gotten her hair done at the salon, so that night she'd slept with a turban of toilet paper wrapped around her head, to keep it from flattening out. Her white denim shorts almost reached her knees because she always felt her thighs were flabby, but she made sure the shorts shaped her butt just so. My mother was ready to strut her stuff.

Jean led us to a picnic table where a balding gentleman with a beard and a paunch belly was setting up his cookware. Next to him was a boy my age who looked just as unhappy as I felt. I could see in the boy's eyes that he had also been unwillingly dragged to this outing, where both his father and my mother could find love or, most likely, lust.

"Well, hello there!" The man was about six feet tall and had the demeanor of a circus clown. "Let me help you with that." He took the cooler from my mother's hands and set it on the table, then extended his hand to my mother. "Roy. I'm Roy Hutchins."

"Thanks. I'm Jean Kurchowski."

"You certainly are," Roy replied as his eyes glided up and down my mother's body. Roy put his arm around the boy, who promptly shrugged it off. "This is my son, Cal."

"Hi there, Cal," my mother said with a phoniness that was making me ill.

"Say hi, Cal." Cal waved with a disinterested, limp wrist and Roy frowned at him. He slapped Cal in the head and yelled, "Say hi, you little shit." My mother's painted smile quickly faded. She picked up the cooler and shrieked to no one in particular, "Barbara, there you are. Come on, C.C."

She fled Roy as I tried to keep up behind her. "Hey, where ya all goin'?" Roy yelled after us.

Jean found us another table to set our food on. This time there was a woman situated there. She was slightly older than my mother and slimmer, with orange-dyed and permed hair. She wore a pin on her dress that said, "Need a hug?"

"Mind if we join you?" Jean asked.

"No. Not at all. I'm Charlotte."

"I'm Jean. This is my daughter, Caroline." I waved and politely said hello. I was afraid Jean might have taken a parenting lesson from Roy.

"Is this your first time at one of these things?" Charlotte asked.

"What gave me away?"

"The sports stuff. Most women only bring that if they have sons. Plus, your make-up. I don't mean to criticize, but you're looking a little eager."

"Does it show that much?"

"Honey, I've been coming to these things for years. Don't worry. The men won't notice, I'm sure. They never notice anything. I've never seen a bigger bunch of boobs who only care about boobs."

Jean attempted to downplay her longing for companionship. "I only came because I'm curious; not to meet anybody, really. If I meet someone nice that would be great, but it's not necessary, by any means. I'm perfectly content being alone." She placed her hands on my shoulders. "I mean with C.C."

Charlotte smiled. "Sweetie, relax. It's okay to admit you need somebody. Who doesn't want someone to grow old with? Nobody likes to be alone, and if they say they do, it's only because they're gay and haven't come out of the closet yet. Come on, I'll introduce you to some people."

Charlotte took my mother by the arm and led her into a huddle of a half dozen men and women who were all pretty unappealing, physically. I would eventually learn that they weren't attractive intellectually, either.

Left to my own devices, I now had to figure out how to waste four or five hours. I decided to sit under a tree. I found a beautiful maple and laid down in the safety of its shade. Just as

I was drifting off for a nap that I deemed would take up most of my time there, Cal stood over me. I sat up.

"What do you want?" I asked. He shrugged. It seems this was a typical form of communication for Cal. He then spent an uncomfortable minute looming over me, until I said, "Sit down if you want." Cal did and we sat there like Charlie Brown and Lucy against the tree. We didn't converse for a few minutes; we only stared out at the patchwork families that milled about the meadow like shorn sheep.

"I hate coming here," Cal finally said.

"How often do you come to these?"

He sighed and swiped at the blades of grass. "Too often, like every other week for the past year. My dad's such a loser."

I was apprehensive to opine, but it seemed like Cal wanted somebody to agree with him. "He seems kind of mean. Does he always hit you like that?"

"That's not my dad."

I was confused. Cal had to explain it to me in detail, and even then it was kind of tough to understand. It seems his mother had never married his father. They were supposed to get married, but a week before the ceremony she revealed that she was pregnant. Cal's father's parents had forced him to call off the wedding for some bizarre religious reason. His mother decided to have Cal anyway. Cal's father secretly kept in touch, even though their relationship was dead. Cal described his father as milquetoast. That was the first time I'd ever heard that phrase. I thought it was a good one. Apparently, Cal's father still lives at home with his parents who feel a need to keep a close eye on him.

Meanwhile, Cal's mother had married Roy Hutchins, the head-slapper, when Cal was three. Four years later, his mother divorced Roy to marry her boss. Cal said that he and Roy had never been close, but Roy paid him twenty dollars to go to these functions because he considered himself too old to meet a woman without kids.

Cal secretly thinks that Roy can't have kids of his own, which might explain why Cal's mother had to sleep with the boss. Cal called it "shooting blanks." This was the first time I'd heard that phrase, as well. Cal was teaching me a lot, and it dawned on me that boys might actually have something to offer.

It also dawned on me that I was feeling something inside that I'd never felt before. I self-consciously noticed the smile that wouldn't leave my face. Suddenly I was playing with my hair a lot, pulling locks across my cheek to place in my mouth. I couldn't stop batting my eyes as I looked into his. My God, I had a crush!

I was stricken with fantasies about Cal leaning in to kiss me, right here, under this tree. I thought he was actually going to at one point, but he'd only lost his balance. Thankfully, he didn't catch me puckering.

Before I knew it, three and a half hours had passed and we hadn't budged from our spot. I wanted it to go on forever, but Jean stepped over to inform me that we were leaving. I told her to give me a minute so I could say goodbye to Cal. While Jean returned to her circle of new friends, I returned my gaze to Cal.

As the seconds ticked and tension mounted, we could each feel the moment stretch into an eternity. I didn't want to just kiss him, I wanted to make out. I didn't even know what making out really was, except for tidbits I'd overheard older girls whisper about in the hallways at school, but those tidbits I'd heard about were what I wanted to do.

"Caroline!" Jean screamed from a distance. "Let's go."

Cal said, "You going to come next time?"

It hadn't occurred to me. I looked over at Jean; she was laughing and scribbling phone numbers down. "I think so."

"Cool." Cal jumped to his feet and held out his hand. He helped me up and then quickly gave me a peck on the lips. It wasn't what I wanted, but it was nice and meaningful. "See ya," he said as he turned and ran off. I couldn't believe that I was actually looking forward to returning to a "Parents without Partners" meeting with Jean.

On the car ride home I couldn't contain the ga-ga, gooey feeling I had about Cal - his dark, messy hair and his chocolate-brown eyes; the slight, upturned nose with a speckling of freckles. He was so cute.

"I guess YOU had a good time," Jean stated knowingly.

"It was okay."

"Nice people, right?"

"Whatever." I needed to appear indifferent, for fear that she had gotten the better of me this go around. "When's the next one?" I asked in a tone that made it seem as if it could still be annoying.

"Next week."

Inside, I was ecstatic. On the outside, I kept my cool. Knowing I was going to see Cal again made me realize the week would seem slow. The anticipation of wondering whether our relationship would take the next step to maybe using our tongues filled me with both dread and excitement. I felt a new surge of adventure inside me. Boys hadn't been yucky for a while, but now they were becoming a welcome challenge, a conquest. My desire and enthusiasm to further the experiment gave me a sense of feeling independent and mature.

And then, Jean shattered my fantasy…

"At our house." What did she mean "at our house"? It seemed that Parents without Partners charged fifteen dollars a person to pay for the cost of securing the location and cleaning up. Jean thought this charge was outrageous and suggested to her new friends that they instead should gather at somebody's house. A charge of five dollars a head and a food item should be enough to meet the demands of the get-together.

And Jean offered to host first, at our house.

As I surmised, Roy Hutchins was not included in this invitation, so my romance with Cal came to a fast and bittersweet end. However, I still remember back to that first kiss fondly.

—— Chapter Six ——

THE COST OF
CHEATING

From the very first day I met him when I was eleven,
Greg Mace was the love of my life. He was thirteen and already
in junior high school, but even at that awkward age, when kids
are riddled with pimples and adolescent perversity, Greg was
gorgeous in every way. Beth and I were riding our bikes
through "Dead Man's Woods," the only part of the
neighborhood that had yet to be turned into a prosaic, suburban
development. There wasn't a lot to it, just a couple of acres
sparsely populated by trees separating my street from the busy
county road. As far as I knew, no corpses had been discovered
there, but legend was that a bullet had been found years back.

No doubt this alleged bullet had been tied to an alleged body, or so the rumor probably spread. Since "Found Bullet Woods" didn't sound sinister enough, "Dead Man's Woods" was the coined name.

Several cliques of children could be found in the woods at any given time. Pre-teens streaked their Schwinn bikes around the paths in third gear. Junior High kids were the ones smoking cigarettes, sipping beers stolen from some father's refrigerator, and generally acting obnoxious. They would hang out near the High School kids, thinking their obvious and repugnant behavior would lead to an invitation. The High School kids would drink and smoke themselves goofy, then make fun of the kids in Junior High.

As Beth and I cycled through the woods, Greg Mace's best friend, Vinnie the Schneak, jumped out from behind a tree screaming an exuberant "Ha!" Startled, I fell off my bike, skidding across dirt and stones. My elbow and shin were scraped up. Vinnie the Schneak, a pale, unctuous, wiry clown, stood over me, laughing. I held my hand over my eyes to block out the sun as I looked up at him with my best war-face. After immediately assessing the situation, I planned a swift kick to the family jewels as payback, but as I raised my foot, an empty beer can hit Vinnie the Schneak square in the head. It must have hurt, because he stopped laughing and turned around rubbing the back of his skull.

Greg stepped forward. "Moron!"

"What the hell'd you go and do that for?" Vinnie wailed.

"Help her up."

"The crazy lady's kid? She's, like, retarded or something." This coming from the kid flunking remedial nose-picking.

"Help her up," Greg demanded.

"Screw you, Mace." Vinnie the Schneak walked away.

Greg put his hand out and lifted me up. He had dark features. His hair was shiny and well-combed, and he had piercing, super-blue eyes that I absolutely lost myself in. Although he was only thirteen, he looked as if he could already grow a beard. Greg was older, crazy handsome, and he had just defended my honor. In that instant, I had a serious crush.

Unfortunately, I didn't have breasts yet, so I knew there was no way for me to compete with the girls his age - but, that didn't stop me from flirting. Unfortunately, aside from breasts, I was also lacking in the tools of seduction.

"I'm not retarded," I informed him, as if the Schneak's accusation needed to be clarified. He smiled at me. I'd just made a complete ass of myself and he should have laughed right in my face, but Greg was a very polite young man.

For the next two years, almost every afternoon I would ride my bike into "Dead Man's Woods," just for a glimpse of Greg Mace. Sometimes I'd see him, sometimes I wouldn't. We never spoke. I just needed confirmation that he hadn't moved away.

By the time I reached 10th Grade, Greg Mace was a senior. Naturally, he was quite popular and nearly every girl in school gossiped about him. If someone haphazardly mentioned that Greg was romantically interested in someone, word spread like wildfire and every girl in every class would get a faraway, dreamy look in her eyes. The odd thing though, was that Greg never dated. While most guys not half as handsome as Greg were using their girlfriends' uvulas as punching bags, he was always walking the halls alone.

"I wonder if he's gay," Beth said, as she passed a bong my way. We were in my bedroom, which had been stripped of all Rick Springfield and Phil Collins posters, only to be replaced with Nirvana and The Cure. We had exactly three hours after school to get stoned and smoke cigarettes before Jean returned from work.

"He's not gay." I nearly choked on the hit.

"I'll bet he's gay," she insisted.

"He won the top athlete award, as a senior! You think they give that to gay men?" How could she argue with that?

"Of course not."

"Okay, then." I knew that wasn't the end of it, because Beth loved playing devil's advocate.

"Unless they didn't know he was gay."

"How could you not know if someone's gay?"

"How do we know if he's straight?" Damn! She went with the old "If you can't prove either, there has to be a possibility" stratagem. Beth was a clever adversary.

There was no proof, no stories. Not even the slightest rumor had spread about some girl fooling around, much less having sex, with Greg Mace.

I smiled smugly. "I can prove it."

Beth sat up. "C.C. Kurchowski! Did you have sex with Greg Mace?"

"No. Don't be stupid. But I would, if he asked me to."

Beth baited me. "Why don't you ask him? For twenty dollars, I'll bet you won't pick up that phone and ask him out."

She dared me and she dared me good. I gave it a long thought, but the pot must have drifted my mind somewhere else, because the next thing I knew Beth was shaking my leg, asking repeatedly, "Do you? C.C.? Do you?"

"Do I what?"

"Have his number?" The moment I'd gotten home after seeing Greg for the first time in the woods, I'd called the operator to find out his exact address and telephone number, then promptly memorized both. I was able to spit the number out as if it were my own.

"923-4088." I still didn't comprehend exactly what it was we were talking about as Beth picked up the phone and dialed.

"What are you doing?" I demanded to know. She waited for a voice to answer. I pleaded with her to stop, but she kept me at bay. To be honest, it wasn't much of a fight, but at that age you're supposed to act like you don't really get gushy over a boy.

I heard the receiver on the other end pick up.

"Hello?"

"Is Greg Mace there?" Beth asked.

"This is Greg. Who's this?"

"This is Caroline Kurchowski," and then she threw the phone in my lap. To her amazement, I was bold and brave. I went straight for the jugular and asked him out. No small talk, just right to the point. If I was going to be rejected, I wanted it quick, like a tetanus shot.

Unexpectedly, he didn't say no. In fact, he told me that he'd had a crush on me since that first day in the woods. Suddenly we were conversing breezily. Not to feel left out, Beth interjected with wild gestures and loud whispers, urging me to ask the question that had prompted the call. Finally, after several annoying prodding pokes to my arm, I asked him why he didn't seem to have any girlfriends or dates. He said he was scared of being rejected. I thought that was so cute.

Greg Mace and I were boyfriend and girlfriend for the next two and a half years. Two years, seven months and nineteen days, to be exact. He was always a fun guy and genuinely decent. He had a slight effeminate quality to him, but he was in no way gay. I found that out on October 1, 1992, when we both lost our virginity. We were in his station wagon, parked by the ballpark at about ten at night. We had already been going out for about three months, but I'd told Beth right after Greg had taken me on our first date that I knew he would be the one.

That night, October 1st, was magical. I kept tugging at his jeans and he kept fighting me. He told me we needed to wait longer, but I didn't want to wait. I wanted to experiment. I wanted to have fun. I also wanted to get back at my mother. This was a perfect chance for me to be bad, and thereby upset Jean. I didn't hesitate.

Understandably, the entire act didn't last long, but I truly loved Greg and it made the night special. With practice we both got better at it, but I will never forget that first time. After Greg dropped me off at home and I skipped up the walkway to my front door, I smirked at the response I would get from Jean. I assumed she would notice that I was suddenly more worldly, sophisticated, and mature.

Jean was sitting on the couch watching "The Golden Girls" as she worked on a needlepoint project of a wintry scene with a sleigh and cabin. It amazed me that not two inches in front of her on the coffee table sat a pile of bills and unopened mail. She could needlepoint while she watched television, but she could never get any junk out of the way.

I leaned against the doorway of the den with my arms crossed, thinking this made me seem more adult. I couldn't wipe the smile off my face. I cleared my throat.

Jean glanced up at me. There was a pause as I anticipated the anger that must have been building up inside of her. Then she went back to her stitching.

"Looks like you had a good time," was all she said.

"I did," I said, pushing the conversation further. She didn't respond. "Greg and I were at…"

"Shush, honey, I'm watching."

I ran upstairs to my bedroom, peeved that I'd been unable to upset her. Sure, I could have come right out and screamed, "Greg and I did it!" but that ruins the fun of the game. It is the daughter's job to keep the secret and the mother's job to be nosy. Jean was not playing her part! Unfortunately, had I revealed my secret to her that night, I never would have been mortified in front of the entire neighborhood later on…

About six months after Greg and I initiated ourselves into adulthood, we were spending every free moment together. I convinced myself that it was an omen when we were assigned the same Spanish class, but it was really only because I was a better student. Greg hadn't begun taking a language class until his sophomore year, while I'd started in junior high. By the time I was in high school, I was in my third year of Spanish alongside Greg.

Mrs. Suzanne Milner was our teacher. She was nearing forty and wore nothing but peasant dresses that she'd probably bought in the sixties. Most kids thought it was because she wanted to appear cool and hip, but there were those of us who knew it was because she was a tad flabby and wanted to hide her belly.

Mrs. Milner constantly acted flaky and waved her arms flamboyantly in front of the room, cracking jokes, trying pathetically to be like her students. Her act was tiresome, but Spanish was the one class I couldn't wait to go to, because Greg was in it.

One day I asked Greg for an assignment that I hadn't completed, all because of my mother's frugality. Unwilling to pay for a plumber, Jean had decided to fix a slight leak in the toilet herself. For some reason unbeknownst to me, Jean was removing the toilet seat with a monkey wrench. I questioned why she needed to remove the toilet seat at all, but she just grunted that she knew what she was doing.

After two strenuous tugs at the bolt, she lost her grip and smashed the wrench into the side of the commode. The hole she made was gaping, and now instead of a small leak, water was gushing from the toilet like the Hoover Dam had busted open. In the end, the new toilet and the plumber to install it had cost nearly ten times as much as she would have paid if she hadn't been so stubborn. Moreover, due to the commotion of cleaning up and yelling at her for being so cheap, I'd neglected to do the assignment for Spanish.

Personally, I didn't think it was such a big deal. The homework was merely a review of material for an upcoming test. It wasn't to be handed in or graded, and would not be reflected in our report cards; we were just going to go over it in class. For that reason, I felt no need to hide what I was doing, which was copying Greg's answers onto my paper during lunch.

Unfortunately, my English teacher, the monumentally rotund Mr. Shuttleworth, didn't feel the same way. He ripped both pieces of paper from my hands and brought them down to Mrs. Milner. I chased him through the hallway, asking him why he wanted to make an issue out of what seemed like a trivial incident. Shuttleworth didn't answer, so I stood there and watched the 320-pound man in a sleeveless sweater vest waddle into Mrs. Milner's classroom.

For the final half-hour of lunch, I sat in the cafeteria pondering my fate. I wasn't concerned about myself. I worried only for Greg. He had received a baseball scholarship to St. Johns University and I didn't want to mess that up for him.

I caught Greg outside Mrs. Milner's room before he entered. I told him what had happened, that he should plead ignorance, and I would take the fall by claiming I'd stolen the assignment from his notebook.

He said, "Let's wait and see what happens."

The Cost of Living

Greg slipped inside as I breathed deeply. I closed my eyes and entered the room only to be blocked by a firm figure. That figure was Mrs. Milner, glaring down at me. She didn't wait for me to say anything. Her teeth were clenched as she spoke.

"You think I care what you do? If you want to ruin your life, that's just fine! But you don't screw up the life of someone as good as Greg Mace along with it! In my eyes, you're garbage!"

I couldn't believe it. Not only was it apparent that Mrs. Milner had a crush on my boyfriend, but my teacher had just called me garbage! I was dumbfounded. In a daze, I took my seat next to Greg. He leaned over to me.

"Did she just say what I think she said?"

All I could do was nod. In a way, I wanted my boyfriend to stand up and defend his distressed damsel, but I also knew that he was already in enough trouble and it was my fault.

I went straight home that afternoon and sobbed on my bed. I wanted Jean to come home so badly. I wanted to tell her about how my teacher had humiliated me in front of the whole class and Greg Mace. Of course, I would also have to mention the so-called cheating, but that was really Jean's own fault due to the toilet fiasco.

By the time she pulled her station wagon into the driveway, I'd gone through an entire box of tissues. She came through the front door yelling her patented greeting, "I'm home!" It was something that had always made me cringe, but this time I was relieved. I yelled to her, "I'm up here."

"What's wrong, sweetheart?" I collapsed into her arms. I explained to her the assignment and Mr. Shuttleworth and Mrs. Milner and, most importantly, the "garbage" comment. She stroked the back of my head, calming me down. She tried to tell me that I shouldn't worry so much about what other people think, but in my opinion that was a typical motherly response to an irrational, teenage situation. Then I realized whom this tidbit of advice was coming from. "The Crazy Lady of Linden Drive" never worried about what others thought! It was the single principle by which Jean lived, and suddenly I admired her for it.

The next morning I tried to push the incident out of my mind, but as Spanish class drew near I became panicked. I thought about skipping out on the period, but talked myself into confronting Mrs. Milner head on. I wasn't going to let this pseudo-hippy chick in a mid-life crisis intimidate me. With my head held high and the utmost decorum, I took my seat in the middle of the class and began taking my test. Periodically I caught Mrs. Milner looking in my direction, and I set my eyes right on hers. After the third time, she refrained from staring at me as if I were a criminal.

Halfway through the test, when I realized I was probably going to ace it and get the last laugh, the pain stemming from the previous day's ruckus was dissipating. It was right around this time that the classroom door burst open. In walked Jean, dragging behind her an extra-large green Hefty bag. I threw my face down on the desk to hide.

Mrs. Milner asked, "Can I help you?"

"I just wanted to clear something up." Jean poured the contents of the Hefty bag onto Mrs. Milner's desk. There was rotten fruit and vegetables, eggshells, grease, containers, uneaten food and a plethora of unidentifiable items. Thinking back, I realize now that I should have been ecstatic that she'd finally cleaned out the refrigerator. However, I was too busy praying to the gods to strike me down where I sat.

"This, is garbage," Jean pointed out.

Mrs. Milner, stunned, replied, "I can see that."

Jean strolled over to me, grabbed me by the elbow and lifted me out of my seat. "This, is Caroline Kurchowski. She is a human being. She has feelings."

To accentuate what had just been stated, Jean walked back to Mrs. Milner's desk and pointed at the pile she'd poured out.

"Garbage." She marched back to me. "Caroline Kurchowski. Do you see the difference?"

Mrs. Milner stood up. "Mrs. Kurchowski, if we can discuss this…"

"There's nothing to discuss. Do you see the difference, is all I need to know."

Mrs. Milner softly replied, "Yes. I see the difference."

"Good!" Jean walked purposefully to the classroom door, and as she made her exit, she said, "Get some new clothes and grow the fuck up."

After she was gone, there was about three minutes of silence. Then Mrs. Milner ran from the room in tears. Five minutes later, the vice-principal arrived to supervise the rest of the exam.

Beth drove me home that afternoon, trying hard to keep me from seething. How could my mother do this to me? It was bad enough that she'd gone to my school to fight my battle without telling me first, but the manner in which she'd accomplished it was beyond normalcy. Now, not only did our neighborhood know about my mother the crazy lady, but the whole school district was clued in.

Since my mother had excused herself from work that day to pull her stunt, she was already home when Beth and I arrived. I stormed into the house with Beth behind me. I screamed at Jean, asking how she could possibly do such a stupid thing. I wanted to know what part of her insane brain had prompted her to load up a bag of garbage, drive it to my school, and dump it on my teacher's desk. She insisted that she was the mother and she did not have to explain anything to her child.

The fight escalated to the point where I ran through my cliche adolescent arguments about needing freedom and space, how I was an adult now and should be treated as such. Jean's response to this was to ground me for a month. I informed her that she couldn't ground me anymore and told Beth to drive me away.

"Beth, don't you drive anywhere," Jean instructed.

Beth, at this point, was desperate to flee the scene. She told my mother, "I don't mean to be disrespectful, Mrs. Kurchowski, but you can't tell me what to do."

"Oh, yes, I can!"

For me, this was a normal fight. For Beth, it was the ultimate terror. She grabbed her keys and bolted out the door. I quickly followed as Beth jumped into her car. I tried to open the passenger door, but it was locked. Beth was frightened and froze for a moment. I pleaded for her to open the door. Finally, she reached over and pulled up the button. I got in the car and Beth shifted into drive, but before she could pull away, Jean burned rubber in her station wagon and cut Beth off.

Fuming, I got out of the car and screamed at Jean. "Are you nuts? What is wrong with you?"

"You're not going anywhere! You think you're all grown up now? You think you don't need me?" At this point joggers and cars were stopping in front of our house to witness the commotion.

I yelled back at her, "You don't even know me! You know nothing about me!"

"I know EVERYTHING about you! October 1st! October 1st!"

I staggered backwards. It was as if her words were pummeling me like a boxer, but I gained my composure and acted as if I didn't know what she was talking about. "What does that mean?"

"If you don't know, it couldn't have been very good! That's the day you lost your virginity! October 1st!"

The neighbors were drifting out of their houses now as if being drawn by the second coming of Christ. I thought back to October 1st, and realized that if only I had rubbed it in her face that very night, I wouldn't have been humiliated in front of the world now.

"You read my journal?"

"I don't need to read your journal. I can read you."

Gazing out at the crowd around us, I felt so isolated.

"You are such a fucking, crazy bitch!" I ran into the house.

"Don't you walk away from me!" Jean followed me inside.

Later I would learn that Beth had been stuck in the driveway for a couple of hours before Jean returned to move her station wagon out of the way.

I locked myself in my room as Jean stood outside the door and berated me. I glanced outside the window for a moment, only to see throngs of people pointing at my house and laughing. I blasted my stereo as loud as possible, to drown out all the noise and thoughts that were scrambling around my brain.

Then, I'm not sure why, but something kept sticking in my head. Jean had said it outside, but it seemed so benign at the time. I could see her face clearly now, screaming "You think you don't need me?" That is what this was all about. She knew that night I'd walked into the house on October 1st that I'd had sex, but she wasn't ready to acknowledge it. There I was, pushing the subject, wanting to share it with her for my own perverse reasons, but in actuality I had been sharing less and less of my life with her for quite some time. I'd been stuck in a routine of going to school, getting stoned with Beth in the afternoons before my mother came home, and then going out each night with Greg. On weekends I was gallivanting from place to place, partying with friends while Jean sat in the empty house alone.

I thought back to the day when Jean had given me my journal. She'd said to me, "It's just you and me, kiddo."

That's all Jean had had for ten years, just the two of us. She was afraid to let go. She'd poured garbage on my teacher's desk because it was her way of saying she didn't want to be excluded from my life for fear of having to move on with her own. And all I was doing was making it harder for her.

That next Saturday I went with her to several garage sales, and then we shared an Early-Bird dinner at the Szechuan Palace – with a "2 for 1" coupon.

— Chapter Seven —

THE COST OF
GOING TO PROM

I was the most popular girl at the prom. I don't say that because I need to give my ego a boost or because that's how I want to remember it. I say that because it's the absolute truth, and I owe it all to Jean Kurchowski. If not for the gown that Jean had gotten for me, all eyes wouldn't have been on me that whole night. I am forever embedded in the minds of those who attended the senior prom, Class of 1993, and the minds of those who heard about it.

To be perfectly clear about one thing, Greg never actually asked me to the prom; it was just assumed by everybody in our high school that we would be attending together. In fact, I'd made the same assumption. I had gabbed on about it for weeks before realizing he had never formally inquired as to my availability.

I peppered our conversations with fantastic plans that included a limousine, a motel room, a fake driver's license, and liquor. Not once did Greg shoot down my ideas, but then again he hadn't agreed to them either. He would merely gaze around the room with a slight nod as I rambled on. Naturally, I took his nodding as acknowledgement. I was extremely excited and honored to be going to the senior prom, especially since I wasn't even a senior.

Two weeks before the big night, I ran to the front door just as Jean was arriving home from work. "I need to get my dress!" I bombarded her with detailed information before she could put down the overstuffed canvas shopping bag she used as her briefcase. "The other girls are all buying at Bennet's Formals. I need three hundred dollars. I have to order it today because they need a week to hem it and then I have to have another fitting to make sure they didn't make a mistake, which I'm sure they won't, but then I need to find some shoes to go with it so if everything is okay with the dress I can bring it around with me to the shoe stores..." I kept talking in the hopes that she didn't hear me say "three hundred dollars," hoping she might hand over her credit card in response to my contagious enthusiasm. I was wrong.

The Cost of Living

"Don't you worry about a thing, sweetie. I've already worked it out," she said with the distinct odor of cheapness.

"Worked what out?" I asked in fear. My mood balloon had just burst. I had been in this situation countless times before, and knew I was in for disappointment.

"Let's get in the car."

"Mom, I don't want to buy my prom dress off the rack at Flora & Bailer's Bargain Basement!" I whined, but the way my body hunched over in complete deflation, a whine was totally appropriate.

"I'm not getting you your prom dress at Flora & Bailer. Your dress will be an original. You won't have to worry about walking into your prom and seeing some other girl wearing the exact same gown. Yours will be unique. There will be no other one like it in the world." She sounded like Robert Preston in "The Music Man." Nevertheless, I was forced to go through the motions, hoping that this time my mother would actually do the right thing.

Unheralded in the fashion world, my mother's wacky friend, Charlotte, dabbled in design. Her basement was filled with "Charlotte's Creations." For example, there was the floral bikini. This consisted of a top made up of a rope with two large daisies and another rope with several smaller daises for a bottom. The entire thing was spray-painted orange. Of course that wasn't nearly as bad as the clam bikini, which I believe warrants no description other than to say there were three clam shells to hide specific anatomical parts.

There were beer top hair clips and pillowcase purses. Charlotte mastered in accessories made from junk. There was no doubt that the pieces were creative. There was also no doubt that nobody in their right mind would ever buy such atrocities. Of course, Jean is not someone who is in her right mind.

My mother had asked Charlotte if she could purchase one of Charlotte's creations for my special night. It seemed as though Jean had made her own assumption about Greg taking me to the prom. Charlotte, apparently, had decided that this would be a great opportunity to showcase her work. I could see the twinkle in her eyes as she daydreamed of all the 17 year olds who were going to pound on her door the next morning, demanding their own "Charlotte's Creations."

"Caroline, this is probably a bigger thrill for me than it is for you," Charlotte said. There was no doubting that she was right. In fact, this was not a thrill for me at all. Unless you define thrill in an amusement park sort of way, as in "the roller coaster was such a thrill, I barfed my cookies on the loop-de-loop."

Sensing the potential windfall and being the shrewd businesswoman that she was, Charlotte offered to give me the gown. She waved her arm across a rack of dresses and told me to choose. I looked at Jean for help, thinking there was no way that she would let me attend the prom in any of these after seeing "Charlotte's Creations" up close - but all Jean could see was the three hundred dollars she was about to save. The smile on her face said it all. She nodded for me to choose.

Not being able to bear the thought of hurting Charlotte's feelings, since she truly was a nice lady and perhaps my favorite out of all of Jean's goofy friends, I forced myself to finger through the gowns. Most of the dresses were made from old clothes that were ripped apart to create new designs. The blue dress had several shades of blue, the red dress was splashed with pink and orange, and the green dress, well, it was just ugly. All of them were sewn with rhinestones, chiffon, lace, or a combination thereof. None of the dresses were discreet. They all screamed, "Look at this person! She can't dress herself."

The last dress on the rack was the closest thing to not being abominable. It thankfully had only one color to it, a pale shade of pink. Ruffles, which seemed to rise at least a foot, aligned the V-neck. I snatched it up. Charlotte seemed a little disappointed.

"Do you think you'll be noticed in that one?" She meant did I think her dress would be noticed.

"Pink is my favorite color," I lied.

"Well, a lot of these have pink in them," she tried to explain.

My mother was no help. Jean thought I should get a dress that incorporated as much material as could fit on one person's body. After all, the dress was free. Think how much she'd be ahead!

For a week, the dress hung from my closet door. I tried to imagine ways I could make it look at least slightly better. Unfortunately, I was not a whiz with a sewing needle. I figured I could pin the ruffles down so they weren't swallowing my face, and then just make the best of it. I knew I wasn't winning any "Best Dressed" awards at the prom, but it wasn't completely hideous, either. Or so I kept telling myself.

The day of the prom, I had my hair and nails done, then went home and put on small amounts of make-up. Everything was done in tiny doses so as not to attract attention to the dress. I waited in my room for Greg to arrive before making my entrance. Since I was already feeling vulnerable, I didn't want to give Jean a chance to criticize how I was presenting myself.

When the doorbell rang, I waited a few moments before greeting Greg in the hallway. Jean was already taking Greg's picture. He looked incredibly handsome in his gray tuxedo with black tie and cummerbund.

When Greg saw me step into the room, his eyes grew wide. Was it because I was beautiful, or was it the Glenda the Good Witch fairy dress I was wearing?

"That dress is... interesting, Caroline." Question promptly asked and answered.

Then Jean chimed in. "Oh, C.C., why did you pin down the ruffles?"

"They covered my face," I said through my teeth. For just one night, I didn't want to hear anything negative.

"But that's what makes the dress work so well." Silly me.

Before Jean could take another Kodak moment, I grabbed Greg by the hand and dragged him outside. I was muttering under my breath, so it took a minute to realize there was no limousine. Instead, Greg had driven his parent's beat-up station wagon. You could smell the exhaust as the engine puttered in idle.

"I thought we were getting a limo?"

"I never said anything about a limo. You said we were going in a limo," he explained. It was true, I did say that, but I had assumed that he wanted what I wanted. I would find out that I'd been very wrong.

As we drove toward the high school, Vinnie the Schneak pulled up next to us at a traffic light in his brown Dodge. Greg tried to pretend not to see him, but Vinnie kept honking his horn. Judging by his t-shirt, jeans, and lack of companion, it was obvious that Vinnie the Schneak was not going to the prom.

"Yo, Greg! You really going?"

Greg shrugged, "Yeah, I guess so."

"You guess so? Or maybe you just like wearing a tux out to the bars?"

"Whatever, Schneak." Greg looked at the light. He sighed in frustration that it hadn't turned green yet.

"Listen, Mace, when you get bored, we'll be at the Dock's End having some fun." The light changed and Vinnie the Schneak hit the gas, leaving tire tracks on the pavement as he took off to his own private gathering. It was becoming clear that the prom was Greg's second choice, or maybe even his third choice, after a speeding ticket. It definitely wasn't his first.

Greg and I drove the rest of the way to the prom in complete silence. He pulled the station wagon into the parking lot and turned off the engine. He looked out at the school, which seemed different at night. It didn't look like the place I trudged to every day. As rain drops began to splatter on the windshield, those entering the building picked up the pace. Music blared each time the door opened.

Greg finally spoke. "Are you ready?"

"Are you?"

He turned to face me. "What's that supposed to mean?"

"I get the feeling you didn't want to come here." I didn't want to say it, but I knew if we didn't talk about it, the night would be torturous.

"I don't know, C.C. Me and my friends had this plan that we were going to boycott the prom. We were gonna go out and have our own party instead of paying a hundred bucks a pop here. But then you kept talking about it and... I don't know... You didn't give me much of a choice. And I know you wanted a limo and to get a motel room, but I don't have that kind of money and my parents weren't going to just give it to me."

The Cost of Living

Suddenly I felt sick. I didn't know what I'd been thinking. This wasn't even my prom. I wasn't even a senior. This was Greg's special night and he didn't want a limo and fancy clothes. On top of that he was feeling bad because he couldn't give his selfish girlfriend everything she wanted.

Strangely, I thought to myself, I don't even like limousines. They're ugly. I didn't even care about fancy clothes or corsages or all the hokey prom traditions. I just wanted somebody to splurge on me sometimes, because I'd grown up with a mother who never would.

I apologized to Greg and I gave him a sincere out. I told him that he could drop me off at home and go meet his friends. Greg smiled. Then he kissed me and said, "You ready to go inside?" I smiled back and told him, "Absolutely."

Like a gentleman, Greg opened my door and the two of us raced to the entrance, trying to avoid as much of the downpour as possible. Once inside, I saw the beautiful decorations that adorned the school. There was a bridge that connected the hallway to the gym and a man-made brook babbling beneath it. From my point of view, I could see that the glitter and lights transformed the dreary gym into a majestic dance hall for this one night. It wasn't a Manhattan club, but it was good enough for me. I gave Greg a long, loving kiss and then grabbed his hand to cross the bridge, but before I was able to take two steps, Greg tugged me back.

"You can't go in there like that," he said.

I knew it. I embarrassed him. Greg didn't expect much, but even he was terrified to be seen with me in this dress. I wanted to cry.

"It's this ugly dress," I said. "Isn't it?"

"What dress?"

Confused, I sought my reflection. In the school's trophy case nearby, I found to my utter mortification that the cheap pink dye from the dress had completely run down my legs. The material wasn't just hanging loosely from my body; it was separating at the seams. To top it off, the entire stitched-together piece of shit that my mother called a gown was now transparent. My bra and panties were visible for all to see.

I threw my arms around my body and turned to flee, but Greg grabbed me before I could get out the door. I was sobbing and he was having a hard time consoling me. I was lucky that nobody had seen me yet and I couldn't understand why Greg wouldn't let me leave. Before I could ask, he pulled me into a vacant classroom.

In June of 1993, at the Oldfields High School Senior Prom, a girl not yet mature enough to be a woman crossed over a bridge to the stunned faces of a few and the applause of many. For that fateful night, I, Caroline Kurchowski, attended the Senior Prom wearing nothing but a gray tuxedo jacket for a top and a cummerbund bottom. I was the hit of the ball. I was wearing "Caroline's Creation."

— Chapter Eight —

THE COST OF
A FLORIDA VACATION

"Jean, you got fat."

All we had done since arriving at my grandmother's two-bedroom, first floor apartment in Boca Raton was place our suitcases on the floor and say hello. Before my grandmother offered us anything to eat following our three-hour flight and two-hour layover in Washington, she criticized my mother. This was the beginning of a week that would prove to be eye-opening, cathartic, and downright gut wrenching.

It all started after Greg had gone away to college. He'd received his scholarship to St. John's, but opted to go to Syracuse instead. It saddened me, since the biggest difference between the two schools was that St. John's was a casual cruise down the highway while Syracuse was a solid five-hour journey. To a seventeen-year old in love, the difference is an extreme one. For the first eight months that we were apart, Greg and I romanced each other on the phone and by mail, but the relationship seemed to be waning. Then we decided to try to rekindle our love by going to Fort Lauderdale for Spring Break.

Knowing that Jean would never let me meet Greg in Florida, I needed a plan. I called my grandmother and asked her if my friend Beth and I could stay with her for a week. She didn't sound enthusiastic, but she consented, which was all that mattered. With step one accomplished, I approached my mother for permission and airfare. Much to my surprise, step two took practically zero coercing. Jean thought it was a great idea, especially since she'd seen an ad in the newspaper for half off on Delta. She said she would go ahead and purchase the tickets.

The only problem with my scheme was that I'd neglected to tell her that I only meant for Beth and me to go. Of course, in my head, I hadn't planned on Beth being there either. In fact, I hadn't even intended to tell Beth that she was part of my alibi. I figured that when I landed in Florida I would tell Grandma that at the last minute, Beth had had a family emergency and couldn't make it.

The Cost of Living

Due to my lack of foresight, Jean had purchased a ticket for herself. I ended up having to take a part-time job at a deli just to pay Beth's way and keep from being caught in my web of lies.

My entire flight to Fort Lauderdale was spent trying to figure out how to see Greg without Jean finding out that this had been my plan all along. My mother seemed tense, however. I asked her if she was feeling airsick, but she said she was fine. Beth was inquiring about my grandmother, but I couldn't answer her because I hadn't seen my grandmother since I was eight. Our relationship consisted of meaningless chats on the phone every other month. Jean's mother seemed pleasant enough, though not very interested in us. Then I began to notice that with every question Beth asked, Jean grew tenser.

I knew very little about my mother's mother. What I did know could barely fill an obituary. Cecilia Kurchowski had been born Cecilia Densham on the Lower East Side of Manhattan. She'd moved to Hempstead, Long Island when she married Henry Kurchowski. She gave birth to Jean, and then, according to Jean, her mother proceeded to torment my grandfather until he died of a heart attack at the youthful age of 52. Eventually my grandmother moved to Boca, where she'd been residing for ten years. That was all I knew.

When she opened the door to welcome us, my grandmother looked nothing like I remembered. She apparently had dyed her hair in the past, because it was now snow white. She was wearing a floral print housecoat that hid her weight. It was stained with spaghetti sauce and Thousand Island dressing.

Her first words to my mother as we stood in her living room explained a lot about her.

"Jean, you got fat."

"No, I didn't, Mom. I'm the same weight I've been for the last seventeen years."

"Yeah, you've been fat for seventeen years."

I looked over at Beth. Her mouth was agape.

As my grandmother continued her onslaught, I studied the living room. There were bills piled high on every table, chicken bones kicked underneath the couch, a stack of newspapers and magazines on the chairs. I made a wager with myself that I knew exactly what type of mess I would find inside the refrigerator. It was as if I had never left home.

As I returned my ear to their dialogue, I caught Jean making a feeble attempt to stick up for herself. "Mom, please don't start. Besides, you ain't exactly looking anorexic yourself."

"Me? I only have five more pounds to lose." As my Grandmother lifted her arms to flaunt her body, the flesh drooped off them a good couple of inches toward the floor. She had at least five pounds to lose in each limb.

The Cost of Living

"You have about five pounds to lose in each limb," my mother said. OK, I was thinking like my mother and that scared me, so I decided this would be a good time to lay in the sun and plot my rendezvous with Greg.

Beth and I donned bikinis and struck poses for the male septuagenarians to gawk at. We were the only ones at the pool younger than the invention of the automobile, and we were wearing two-piece suits. The Florida humidity and mugginess began to penetrate my skin in a matter of mere seconds, so I went to cool off in the water. As I dipped my big toe in, some old biddy wearing a bathing cap adorned with daisies squawked at me.

"Read the rules first, deary!"

She was pointing to a sign nailed to the wall of the bathrooms and showers. Listed in no particular order were the rules of the pool. The first stated that you had to shower before swimming. There was no diving, no jumping, and no game playing allowed. No shorts or t-shirts could be worn in the water. In addition, one-piece bathing suits and bathing caps were to be worn by women at all times. The rules were obviously written by old women who didn't like the idea of their husbands ogling young nymphs in their presence. They were out to make us look unattractive.

After being exiled from the pool area, Beth and I decided to explore other fun areas of the seniors' community. The billiard hall was off-limits to anyone under eighteen, we were told to keep off the shuffleboard court for fear of wearing out the pavement, and the movie-house was only for those with resident passes. In essence, there was nothing for two 17-year old girls to do. This gave us all the more reason to find Greg.

Greg had given me his flight and hotel information before I'd left home, but I still had to find a way to get to him without my mother knowing. We couldn't use the excuse that we were going to the mall, since shopping was Jean's forte and she would have insisted on joining us. Although Beth and I both had fake IDs, we certainly couldn't say we were going to a bar. The way I saw it, we had only one option. We had to sneak out after Jean fell asleep and be back before dawn.

Luckily, my mother agreed to sleep on the couch in the living room, so Beth and I shared the extra bedroom. Our plan was to climb out the window of my grandmother's apartment and make a run for it. The best plans are always the simple ones, but my plan ended up becoming far more complicated.

That night, as my Grandmother and Jean were preparing something resembling a meatloaf and mashed potato dinner, I happened to overhear them talking through the vent. At first it was quite boring, mostly about health issues. My grandmother's description of the crust forming on her feet was making me ill - but soon my ears perked up.

"You know who I ran into…" my grandmother said.

"Who?"

The Cost of Living

"Danny." I heard a plate drop.

My Grandmother yelled at my mother, "Jean, all over my clean floor?" Her floor was filthy. It hadn't been cleaned in months and now my dinner was laying on it.

"Just wash it under the faucet," my grandmother instructed, "The girls will never know." I heard water hitting the sink. Now I had to find a way to get out of dinner as well.

After the faucet was turned off, my mother asked, "He lives down here?"

"I ran into him at Publix. He's only a few blocks from here. He bartends somewhere in Lauderdale. I was right about him; he never amounted to anything. He's still an irresponsible child. I don't know why you couldn't hold onto him."

"You just called him a loser. Why would I want to hold onto him?"

"Who else are you going to get?" More and more, I was beginning to understand my mother's childhood and how her thought processes had developed. Sweet old Granny was mean and demeaning.

My guess was that Danny was a former flame of my mother's. I thought this might inspire my mother to look him up and go out on a date. He didn't sound like much, but I knew she needed to be with a man, or at least a contemporary.

Then I heard my mother say, "Let's just drop this now, before C.C. hears us."

"Don't tell me she still believes that nonsense about him being taken away for being stupid?"

My God, they were talking about my father! My father lived nearby and worked in Fort Lauderdale! And his name was... Danny? My mother had told me that my father's name was Lester. Why would she lie to me about something so seemingly insignificant? Was he a mass murderer? Did he molest children? The worse the characteristics my imagination assigned him, the more I wanted to meet him.

Now I had another reason to go to Fort Lauderdale.

By the time my mother was snoring on the couch, it was already eleven o'clock. Beth and I bounded out the window and strolled nonchalantly through the security gate, mindful to greet the guard so he would remember us when we returned.

Greg had rented a red Mustang convertible and was idling in the parking lot of the convenience store across the street. It was only a twenty-minute drive to downtown Lauderdale, but the bars closed at two o'clock, so that left me precious little time to find my father. If he wasn't working in that part of town, or it was his off-night, chances were likely that I would miss him altogether. The window of opportunity was small, but it was the second window I was willing to crawl through that night.

We dropped Beth off at a bar called Jupiter's so she could have some fun. Greg told her where his motel room was so she could meet up with us later on. As we inched along the main strip in bumper-to-bumper traffic filled with rowdy kids, I raced repeatedly from the car up to bouncers outside the bars and asked if a 40-year old bartender named Danny worked there. One by one, I was turned away.

Greg was getting frustrated. We hadn't had sex in months and I knew it was something he'd been anticipating with increasing fervor. I didn't want to deny him, but I wasn't willing to abandon my father-seeking mission just yet. I figured I would apologize to him later in the evening, explaining that I'd wanted my head clear so that all my attention could be focused on him. Guys loved to hear that stuff.

Last calls rang out along the strip and I felt my heart pounding as if two o'clock meant my last breath. We came to the end of a block and before I even reached the bouncer in front of "The Elbow Room," I heard someone shout from just inside, "Hey, Danny! Line up another round of shots."

I peered inside and saw a handsome, tanned man with curly blonde locks and a mustache pouring Jack Daniels into a row of shot glasses. I studied his features, trying to recognize myself in his face. The bouncer tapped me on the shoulder.

"In or out, but you can't stand there."

I signaled Greg to park the car. We entered the bar together and stood in the back against the wall. I didn't know how to approach my father. He had a wicked smile with dimples, and as he flirted with a young, nubile co-ed, he used them for all they were worth.

Greg said, "Maybe this isn't such a good idea." He was getting antsy, and though I completely agreed with him, something inside me needed to speak with this man behind the bar. I wasn't expecting hugs, but I did need to know why he wasn't in my life.

As I walked up to the bar, I was hating Jean all over again. If only she had been honest with me and explained to me what had happened to my father, without the wild tales, I wouldn't have been in such a predicament.

I sat on the stool next to the co-ed and listened in as Danny bragged about himself. He claimed he was a surfing champion from years back, saying that he loved the sea and sand so much, he never wanted to leave. Then, with the charm of a snake, he added, "Besides, with hot looking babes like you coming down half the year, why should I go anywhere?"

This sickened me. I didn't know this man, and I was still only assuming he was my father, but attached to such an assumption is a list of things a daughter doesn't want to hear. A distasteful image popped into my head of him lying in bed in a one room apartment, reading "How to Pick Up Women" by a red neon glow outside his window.

Danny handed the girl her drink. She asked him, "What do I owe you?"

"This one's on me, honeymuffin."

She smiled at him, grabbed the drink and bounced off her barstool. "Thanks," she said, and then disappeared into the crowd to find her friends. Danny snapped his mop-rag in disappointment. It was part of the game. Pretty girls want to drink free and horny bartenders want to get laid. Chalk one up for the pretty girls this round.

Standing on his toes and looking out over the crowd, Danny searched for her, but she was lost. Then he noticed me. He flashed me his crooked smile. "Hey, you!"

If I hadn't overheard his banter with the co-ed, I might have thought, if only for an instant, that he remembered me. However, I was plainly more cynical than naïve. I held up my hand to cut him off before he could get started. "I'm Caroline Cecilia."

"Of course you are."

My name didn't ring a bell in his sun-soaked head. He held out his hand. "Danny. Danny Lowe." I couldn't shake his hand. Not yet, anyway. I was still blocked by how Jean had told me his name was Lester Hargrove. I began having doubts as to the legitimacy of my pursuit. What if this wasn't my father? Was it all just wishful thinking?

"My last name's Kurchowski," I relented.

"No, shit! I knew a Kurchowski. Long time ago. You wouldn't happen to be from the New York area, would you?" It was now obvious that with a name like Kurchowski, this man was at least connected to my mother in some way.

"As a matter of fact, I am." He hadn't put one and one together, but maybe two and two.

"You might be related to her, then. Jean, Jean Kurchowski..." His voice trailed off and his smile waned. Finally, he figured it out, as did I. This was indeed my biological father.

"Doreen?"

Doreen? Who the hell was Doreen? Maybe this wasn't my father.

"My name's Caroline," I informed him.

"So she slighted me on that one, too. She always had to get her way. I ask you, is it too painful to name a child Doreen? That was my mother's name, after all, and she..."

"Don't start bad-mouthing my mother." What was that? What did I say? Was I defending Jean? Danny the bartender smiled at me. He apologized and then asked me what I wanted to drink. I was quickly discovering the benefits of having a father as a bartender. "I'll have a rum and coke." He mixed the drink, flipping bottles in the air and then catching them behind his back. He slid the cocktail over to me. He was trying pathetically hard to impress me. It reminded me of a junior high school adolescent wiggling his ass backwards in a roller rink, showing off the only wheels he was old enough to have.

As I took large gulps from the rocks glass, he leaned on the bar and said, "So, tell me. I want to hear everything about you." The feeling was reciprocated, but I couldn't figure out how to start things off. I didn't want to 'rap,' I wanted answers; but before I could ask any questions, a buxom blonde with leathery skin, wearing a florescent-orange bikini top and teeny white shorts, yelled down from the other end of the bar.

"Dan, what the hell are you doing? Everybody's waiting to be served." Sure enough, I looked down the bar and hands holding bills were stretched out in a row.

"In a minute, honey. C'mere. I want you to meet somebody."

He turned to me, "Betty manages the place."

This was becoming embarrassing. I didn't want to meet his new wife, or girlfriend, or "present squeeze." For just a few minutes, I wanted quality time. After seventeen years, I felt I was entitled to it. But, down strolled the "middle-aged mama" as if she was on a catwalk. The only thing missing was her tiara.

"Betty, this is my daughter." He said this with pride, which angered me. For all he knew, I was a crack whore using him to help me make a score. "Isn't she beautiful?" He tried to touch my face, but I reflexively pulled away from his hand, making an awkward moment worse.

Betty, nodding in my direction, asked, "You're Jean's girl?"

I nodded. I didn't want to make conversation with this sleazy-looking woman and suddenly I regretted the entire night. Then it occurred to me: How did she know my mother? My father must have picked up on this tidbit of information that

Bleach-Blonde Betty had mistakenly revealed, because he abruptly said, "Betty and Jean were friends a long time ago."

"We weren't exactly friends… How's your mother? She break the scale yet?"

Now I really hated this woman. My father screamed at her, "What the hell is wrong with you?"

"What?"

"You don't say that in front of my daughter."

"Your daughter. Ha! You don't know shit about this girl. And I keep telling you, don't you be yelling at me in here!"

I suddenly felt hundreds of eyes looking our way. I decided to finish my rum and coke and make a hasty exit, but as I put the glass to my lips, Bitchass Betty pointed at me and said, "Wait. Is there liquor in that? Do the math, Einstein! She's only seventeen! What the hell are you doing serving liquor to a minor!?"

Just then, a young looking man dressed like a college student produced a badge. He didn't say much, only that he was an undercover cop, my father and I were under arrest, and then some mumbo-jumbo about our rights and such. As he manhandled us out of "The Elbow Room," I yelled over to Greg that I was sorry and I would meet him at the motel. My father kept muttering, "Not again. Don't you boys have anyone better to harass?"

The Cost of Living

At the police precinct the cells were already filled with drunks and hookers, so my father and I were handcuffed side by side to a wooden bench. For the first hour, we didn't speak. I wasn't really concerned about my mother finding out about my latest predicament, since Danny'd told me in the squad car on the ride over that Betty was going to bail the both of us out. He'd also mentioned that he would prefer we didn't say anything about this to Jean, which was my intention all along.

For the final two hours that we were stranded together in that hallway, I got to know my father a little, and little was all there was to know. Dan was an overgrown teenager. He'd never had any aspirations, except to get drunk and get laid as often as possible. He'd met my mother in a bar and told me that she'd been quite rebellious, a real party girl. This took me by surprise. I could describe Jean in many specific ways, but party girl was not one of them. Dan assured me that Jean had been wild because it was a way of getting back at my grandmother, a woman he characterized as "the nastiest bitch with the most negative karma that ever lived." He was right on target.

Finally, after realizing I might not ever have contact with him again, I asked my father, Danny Lowe, why he and my mother weren't still together. I half-expected to hear that she had simply driven him crazy. That would have almost been absolvable.

"I'm sure your mother has told you some ridiculous stories about me and why our marriage didn't work out..."

He could have been right. After all, everything she had told me about my father up to then had been false. Perhaps he wasn't such a bad guy. Maybe, just maybe, all the negative ideas I had about him had been conjured up by the bitterness of a scorned woman. If I'd left the police precinct at that moment, I actually might have liked my father, but he was stupid enough to keep talking.

"Doreen," he said to me, and I didn't bother correcting him, "your mother probably told you she left me. Well, I can tell you this and it's the God's-honest truth - I left her. I'd warned your mother before we got married, when we got married, and after we got married. I couldn't have stressed it enough because I believe in open communication in a marriage."

"Warned her about what?"

"I told her not to get fat. I wasn't going to spend my life with no fat chick. And she knew this."

I laughed. How could I not laugh? My father ran out on my mother because she'd gained weight? And even after seventeen years, he was still blind to his shallowness? Then it hit me: seventeen years. He'd stayed around long enough to impregnate her, which meant he'd left her because she'd gained weight from carrying me.

"You left her because she was pregnant!"

"Hey, quiet down there," a police officer bellowed from his desk.

"I left because she was fat."

The Cost of Living

"You asshole!" The handcuffs kept me from punching him. After struggling with them for a moment, I decided to head-butt him instead. I basically went insane, like a bull gorging a matador.

Dan screamed for help. Two policemen had to wrestle me off of him.

"Danny!" Bouncing-Boobie Betty jiggled down the hall toward us, waving papers. "I bailed you out!" At least she was good for something. The policeman uncuffed us after I promised that I wouldn't attack my father again. All I wanted to do at this point was see Greg, smother him with affection, and then get back to my grandmother's for some much needed sleep. Unfortunately, it turned out to be the night where everything that could go wrong, did.

"Where is she?" I heard her from around the corner. It was Jean and she was enraged. "Where are you holding my daughter? If she's been raped by one of your convicts, I am holding this entire city responsible!"

Ironically, I looked to my father for salvation, but the sound of her voice must have struck a terrible memory from deep within his puny, superficial mind, because Danny's eyes were nearly halfway out of his sockets and he turned a ghostly white.

"Come on, Betty. We gotta go."

I beseeched him half-jokingly, "Take me with you!"

Danny grabbed my release papers from Betty's hand and thrust them into my own. "Sorry, kiddo. Call me if you need me." Then he and Betty scampered the other way, just as Jean appeared from around the corner.

"Caroline!" She ran up to me and threw her arms around me, hugging me tightly. "You're alright!"

"How'd you know where to find me?"

"I've been calling every hospital and precinct in the area. You had me scared silly. Thank God you're alright."

Finally she let go of me, held me by the face and examined me. She was genuinely relieved. She was not the Jean Kurchowski that I had expected. My mother stroked my cheek with the back of her hand. "My little Caroline."

Then she slapped me. "Are you a nincompoop?" THAT was the Jean Kurchowski I'd expected.

Jean drove me to Greg's motel, but only to pick up Beth. I had to explain my reasons for sneaking out of the apartment, which were completely unforgivable since they involved Greg, but I confronted her on her lies about my father as well.

"I didn't lie." As always, she denied it.

"What do you mean you didn't lie?" I didn't want to let her talk her way out of it. "You told me my father's name was Lester Hargrove. It's Danny Lowe. That's lie number one."

She paused to strategically plan her response. "I didn't lie to you. I kept you from finding out the truth."

"What do you think a lie is?"

The Cost of Living

"There's a difference. A lie is meant to hurt you. I wasn't out to hurt you. I was saving you from finding out about him."

"You can rationalize it all you want. It's still a lie." For once, I just wanted to hear, "I'm sorry. I was wrong." Five little words that would have taken all the pain away.

"We'll just have to agree to disagree then." This was a statement Jean often used when she couldn't talk her way out of something. It was a statement I hated because whoever says it initiates the truce, leaving the second party with no choice but to be accepting and amicable, thereby losing the argument. I felt an irrational rage boiling from deep within my soul.

"No, we will not agree to disagree. You told me he was sent out of state for being stupid. I want to know how you could decide not to tell me the truth. He's my father, after all. I should have had the opportunity to find out for myself..."

Jean hit the brakes and my grandmother's car came to a screeching halt. Several cars behind us skidded to avoid us.

"I did not lie to you. If you didn't notice, after spending just a small amount of time with him, he is stupid. For years all he did was get drunk and tell me I was no good and that I was ugly. He didn't just leave me, he left us. He didn't want custody. He didn't fight for you, so don't fight for him."

Tears began to stream down her face. I was ashamed. She had done it to me again; made me feel guilty even though I knew I had a sound argument.

"He didn't want us, Caroline. So, yeah, he's not around because he's stupid."

She couldn't stop sobbing now. Years of being ridiculed by my grandmother and my father had taken their toll on Jean. She was a woman with low self-esteem trying to make our life together work. I placed a comforting hand on her shoulder and she looked up at me, her eyes glassed over from tears.

With a smile, I said, "You have to admit, you stretched the truth a little."

She chuckled, "No I didn't." And I conceded, to make things right between us. "Okay, you didn't."

We pulled up to Greg's motel and it took me several minutes to remember his room. Then my mother suggested that I ask the night clerk. When I found the room, I tried the knob. The door was unlocked, so I pushed it open. It was dark, but I heard some rustling. "Greg?"

"Oh, shit." I heard the bed shake and somebody fall with a thud to the floor. I found the light switch and flicked it on. Greg had his underwear up to his knees. It was disconcertingly evident that he was putting them back on, not taking them off.

"No. Don't tell me…"

"Caroline, listen…" I could see a shadow moving on the wall behind the bed. I craned my neck to try to see what she looked like, but I was almost positive who it was. It was Beth. My heart sank to my stomach. My breathing became short and

I just wanted to escape from the nightmare, but I couldn't leave Beth behind, not with Jean in the car.

"Beth, my mom's downstairs waiting. We gotta go." I turned around so Beth could get dressed. Greg walked up behind me.

"Caroline, I'm sorry. I didn't mean for this to happen! She came back drunk and I was drunk and we were just stupid drunk together…"

"You can do better than that."

"You know, I've been pretty faithful to you so far."

"Pretty faithful? What does that mean, you've cheated on me before?"

"No! But… I mean, to be honest, I was going to suggest we see other people after this week was over anyway." I'm sure that somehow he thought that was a valid excuse.

Beth slipped out the door and went down to the car. She was smart; she wasn't opening her mouth.

"Goodbye, Greg."

"Don't leave like this," he pleaded. "We need to talk about this."

"No, we don't."

Beth didn't say a word on the car ride back to my grandmother's. Jean kept wrinkling her nose, just to let me know she was aware that Beth had been drinking. We returned to my grandmother's as the sun rose. I put Beth to sleep on the couch so my mother and I could share the bed. We needed to be close to each other, at least for that night.

We had five more tense-filled days in sunny Florida, the first three of which were spent in agonizing silence. Although I hadn't confided in Jean about Beth's fling with Greg, her intuition took over and her two-cents had to be contributed.

"I'd be remiss if I didn't say anything."

Although what Beth had done was taboo between friends, Jean let me know that youthful discretions are like uncomfortable shoes: Everybody has at least one in their closet.

After one more day of sulking, I confronted Beth. Before she could explain, she broke down in tears. "The last thing I ever wanted to do was hurt you, C.C." She fell into my arms. "I don't know why I was so jealous of you."

Eventually I would learn that Beth had been envious of my relationship with Greg all along. She hadn't experienced dating and had found it tough being around us. She didn't think that I needed her anymore. I admitted that I'd taken her for granted, letting her drop out of my life except for times when I would use her for my own convenience, like as an alibi for the trip. She had been a horrible friend tonight, but I hadn't been much of one either, for quite some time. I told her that I did need her, and I wasn't lying.

For the remainder of the trip there was an obvious rift between Beth and me. Things were awkward and we barely spoke, instead letting the radio fill the silence between us as we laid out in the Florida sun. It wasn't until the final night that we were able to finally pave the potholes of our friendship. It was my idea to secure some alcohol. It was Beth's idea how to go about getting it.

Across the street from the gates of my grandmother's community, there was a convenience store. We waited outside the store for a not-so-nice looking man to drive into the parking lot. Before long, a beat up red Ford flatbed screeched to a halt right near us. Out of the truck stepped a young man with unwashed hair, a thin mustache, bad acne, and a sweatshirt with the slogan "If you gotta screw, I've got the nut". This was our guy, for sure. We knew we'd be popping the tabs on a couple of brewskies within minutes.

"Hey, Mister," I said in my best small-town Florida drawl.

"What do you little ladies want?" He was inspecting us; maybe to guess our ages, but in any case it was creepy and oogie. And yet, it did not deter me from answering him.

"It's awful hot out here. We're kind of thirsty. Do you think you could buy us a six-pack?"

"What's in it for me?" His eyes bugged open. Judging by his shirt, he no doubt thought this was a stellar pick-up line that he'd conjured up on the spot. He was probably already imagining how he was going to go see his friends later and cackle, "So then I said to them girls, 'What's in it for me?' Can you believe I said that?"

"What do you want?" Beth asked. I got nervous. This was a loaded question and I had never conceived taking it this far just to get a few beers.

He swiveled his head to see if he was being watched. Then he stuck his tongue out the side of his mouth and nodded. "How about showing me some titty?"

I was ready to run in the opposite direction. Beth really wanted beer.

"After you buy us the beer."

He wagged his finger at us, saying playfully, "Now don't you go nowhere now." The double 'now' was precious, but I still wasn't going to flash this junior high dropout.

Once he disappeared inside the convenience store, I turned to Beth and slapped her shoulder. "Are you crazy?"

"Relax. What's a little flash?"

"I am not flashing this guy." I crossed my arms in front of my boobs to emphasize how no one in this godforsaken liquor store parking lot was going to see my babies, not even with x-ray vision.

"Nobody said you had to. Besides, mine are better looking anyway."

The Cost of Living

"Who says? Did Greg say that?" As soon as I'd let that spill from my mouth, I realized I had brought up the very taboo subject we'd been trying to avoid and escape in the first place.

Before Beth could answer, not that she wanted to, Huckleberry returned with a large paper bag. He pulled out one six pack. "This one's for looking at 'em."

Beth reached out to take the beer, but Huckleberry pulled it away. "Uh-uh. Not until I see 'em." Beth sighed and rolled her eyes. Before she could second-guess herself, she pulled her top up. I looked away toward the convenience store and caught the clerk watching. Huckleberry had clearly told him what was about to go down. I let out a disgusted "ugh".

Beth counted to three out loud and then pulled her shirt back down. Huckleberry nodded approvingly. "Nice..." As if he had anything else to compare them to, I thought. Beth grabbed her bounty.

Huckleberry reached back into the bag again and pulled out a second six-pack. "This one's for touching 'em." He dangled the beer like a carrot. Beth grimaced. "Forget it, hayseed."

In that moment, something came over me. I lifted my shirt up. "Here," I announced. Huckleberry reached out and grabbed a breast. Just as he cupped it, I pulled down my shirt forcing his hand away, but in that instant I knew that this unsavory, immature act was my revenge on Greg and my way of standing up to Beth. Of course, it was neither revenge nor standing up for anything; it was merely just unsavory and immature.

"How was that?" I asked smugly, awaiting a response like, "Magnificent! You should be in Playboy with those funbags!" Instead he mumbled, "They're okay." And with that, he handed me my beer and climbed into his truck. Before driving off he stuck his head out the window. "You girls wanna come to a party?"

"No!" We both yelled in unison. Then we looked at one another and began to howl. We couldn't stop laughing as we ran across the street with our beer and re-entered the old folks' ranch. We found ourselves a nice place under the stars on the 17th hole of the golf course, where we proceeded to slurp down our dozen beers. We let the alcohol seep into our brains until we hit each other with barrages of accusations, apologies, and finally, cries of "You're my best friend in the whole wide world." Then we laughed about all the dumb things we had done together, including that we had let some Huckleberry ogle and grope us for two six packs of beer. We laughed until we wanted to throw up and then, having emptied the last can, we staggered back to my grandmother's apartment.

We were loud, too loud. We shushed each other, but not in hushed tones. We were giggly, like school girls. Well, we were still school girls. We probably could have made it to a bed without anyone knowing if I hadn't accidentally knocked Beth over onto the rattan coffee table, which collapsed with ease. This is what woke up Jean and my grandmother.

The lights came on like a prison spotlight, catching me in the act of trying (unsuccessfully) to pull Beth to her feet. We recognized the silliness of how we both must have looked, and spit out huge guffaws as I fell on top of Beth in hysterics.

Jean rushed over to help us both up. "Aww, C.C... What have you girls done?"

"That's how you're going to handle this? They're drunk as skunks!" my grandmother announced.

"Mom, I will handle this," Jean replied firmly but calmly.

"You've never been able to handle anything before," my grandmother snorted.

As I was trying once again to yank Beth to her feet, I suddenly let go and she dropped back onto the broken table. "Now listen here, lady!" I swaggered over to my grandmother like a cowgirl, my arms swinging wildly low to the ground. I was Annie Oakley and King Kong's bastard child.

"My mother has taken enough from you. You abuse her and make her feel like shit and fuck with her head and...and...and, you know, you're not so hot to trot yourself. Did you know that?"

I felt like I was making some sense. It might have been gibberish, but in my head it was verbal gold. "You will cease and desist from this moment on!" (I'm pretty sure I remember this coming out "decease and resist")

My diatribe continued: "This woman raised me. Yes, she did. Raised me from the littlest, little..." I lost my train of thought at this point, but then I became a preacher. "And the Lord will strike you down if you ever say another mean thing to her! You are a hideous monster. And you're old. Yes, you are..."

I threw my arm around my mother, partly to show our solidarity and partly because I needed help standing. My mother, tight-lipped, grinned. Then she started chuckling, trying hard at first to keep it in. Sure, I was drunk, but I had also just defended her for the first time in my life. "It's only you and me, kiddo!" It was my turn to drive that point home.

My grandmother stood in silence for the longest time. Then she pointed at me. "This is what you call good parenting?"

— Chapter Nine —

THE COST OF
OWNING A CAR

"It's nice," I stated less than enthusiastically. It was not nice. The gesture was nice, but the car wasn't.

It was my senior year of high school and I had begged Jean to buy me a used car. I'd sworn, crossing my chest and all, that I would pay for the registration, insurance, gas, and any repairs. It took plenty of coaxing on my part and an extra effort for top grades in school, but Jean had finally given in.

I just never assumed that she would buy a car for me without having me check it out first; and this assumption was correct, because I later learned that she hadn't purchased the car at all. It was given to her.

Jean had posted a notice on her bulletin board at work, for anyone to let her know if a used vehicle was available for purchase. Of course, the word 'cheap' fell in there somewhere. The janitor, Sam, a pleasant, humorous, retired gentleman, who out of boredom had decided to take a job as a custodian to wile away the days, told my mother he had an old Toyota Corona sitting on his lawn that didn't run. He reasoned, "It ain't doin' me any good just sittin' there like that. Heck, I should pay you to take it off my hands."

Well, Jean being Jean, she jumped at that bargain. No matter how much Sam said he'd been kidding about the "paying her" part, Jean insisted that a deal was a deal.

In the end the old man thankfully won out, but Jean was able to cajole him into paying the towing fees to get the car from his lawn to her driveway. "If you were getting rid of it you'd have to get it towed to the junkyard, anyway. So why should I pay for that?" was her argument. The irony of towing the car to her house instead of a junkyard completely escaped her. Jean was still trying to get the best deal she could, and she didn't care if she had to take advantage of an elderly man (who had less money than she did) to do it.

When I returned from school that autumn day, I gathered the wet leaves that sat like mush atop our overgrown grass. In some paradoxical way, when the high winds blew, all the leaves on all the lawns in our neighborhood seemed to end up on our property. They never blew past our lawn, but right onto it. It was almost as if old, withered and decayed things knew where to go when no one else wanted them. I agonized about how I would have to rake all weekend, but then figured it didn't matter much since I had no car to go anywhere, anyway.

Then, as I turned the corner, I saw it. I couldn't make out exactly what it was at first, since it was covered with a yellowed and frayed bed sheet that was spray-painted with giant purple letters "Surprise, Caroline!" As I got closer, I saw that the shape resembled a car - a rusted, dilapidated car. Once I took the sheet off, the color was a light brown with gray spots, no doubt from the sun beating down on unwaxed metal. I couldn't make out whether it had originally been dark brown or red. The back windshield was busted and a thousand small fragments of broken glass sat in the back seat. Three tires were flat, two with dented rims.

Jean excitedly bounded from the house, skipping up to me. "Nice, huh?"

"It's nice." It wasn't nice. It was a wreck. It clearly needed plenty of fixing up and part of our deal was that I was to pay for all repairs. I calculated that by the time the car could be operable, my future husband would be able to buy me a new one.

I closed my eyes for a moment to reflect on my mother's good intentions. She'd given me a car and I wasn't being gracious. I opened my eyes, disappointed to find that the jalopy hadn't magically transformed into something resembling an automobile.

"Here are the keys!" Jean dangled the set in front of my face. I took them from her and sat in the driver's seat. My foot accidentally slid the muddied floor mat forward, revealing a hole about a foot in diameter. I could see not only the driveway, but also a puddle of fluid that was leaking from the transmission. Like any normal teenager would, I noticed right away that the vehicle lacked a radio. I inserted the key and turned the ignition. What I received in return was nothing, not even a cough.

"You can't drive it yet, silly." Yes, silly me. How crazy was I to be given a car and expect it to run? Apparently, Sam the janitor had given my mother a list of reparable problems with the car. The list was long. It included: transmission work, a new starter, spark plugs, brakes, rims, tires, a timing belt, muffler, oil leak, battery, and on and on. Jean snorted that she was sure all of it didn't need to be done to get the car on the road. I of course had my doubts, as well as a growing concern for my safety.

"Mom, I can't drive this," I began to plead my case.

Jean shifted and put her hands to her hips. "Were you expecting a Cadillac?" I definitely had not. I was a young, hip, socially conscious student of the eighties. In other words, I was naïve. I hated Cadillacs and all they stood for, which had something to do with OPEC, pollution and McCarthyism.

"No, but I'd like something that works," I said facetiously.

"This will work, you'll see."

"But I can't afford to fix this up right now. The point was to have a car for my senior year."

"I figured it all out. I'll pay for the repairs now and you can pay me back on a weekly basis until we're square." She had that stupid smile on her face that told me, "This is it, honey. So make the best of it because you ain't gettin' anything better and you can't argue with me."

She put a congratulatory arm around me, but I sensed she was really patting herself on the back. Then she led me inside, remembering first to grab the old "Surprise, Caroline!" bed sheet, which I was sure she would use again for another relevant occasion.

After calling more than thirty auto repair shops, Jean finally received the best deal she thought she could get. Some mechanic had a brother with a friend out of work who could fix the car cheaply, as long as we paid in cash. He promised that "the guy" would get it into shape so it could pass inspection. That was all Jean needed to hear. Or, more to the point, it was what she wanted to hear.

"The Guy" was a sleazy drunk who would chug about a case of beer as he tinkered underneath the hood. Sometimes he would show up; other times he wouldn't. He creeped me out, and if he was in the driveway when I got home I would race into the house and bolt the door. Finally, after almost two months he got the car running. It certainly didn't hum like a well-oiled machine. Actually, it sounded more like belching, although that could have just been "The Guy." The only thing left before my new old car could pass inspection was a rear windshield.

For the next week, Jean phoned every junkyard she could find on Long Island to hunt down a back windshield for a 1972 Toyota Corona. Ultimately she found somebody unloading one for fifty dollars that was "only slightly cracked." She drove out to Riverhead just over an hour away, got the back windshield, and then had "The Guy" install it.

I gazed longingly at my new set of wheels. Suddenly the car didn't seem like such a bad idea. It was cute, in a bohemian-scrap metal kind of way. More importantly, it was my first car, and I wanted to stop and appreciate the moment. Unlike others who might take this for granted, it was important to me. Like Greg had been my first, this was special, too.

Then I thought about Greg and how I wished I could share this with him. I wanted so much to drive to his house and ask him if he wanted a ride, but I hadn't gotten over the pain he'd inflicted on me in Florida. He'd tried to call once or twice since then, and he even sent me a nineteen-page letter, with poems, to apologize for his insipid and insensitive behavior. I wanted to date him again, and almost brought myself to the point of forgiving him, but then I'd imagine myself married to him, looking at his face and thinking, "You screwed my best friend!" I knew his behavior was unforgivable and I'd become extremely wary of men. I had fooled around at a few parties and even had sex with one other boy since breaking up with Greg, but I was nowhere near ready for another relationship.

Musing on this, my moment with my car had passed. Jean broke my concentration when she asked, "Want to take it for a spin?"

I shook my head no. "Tomorrow, when I take it to school." Jean was a little disappointed, but I wanted the first ride to be memorable, and I was remembering too much other stuff at the time.

The next morning I galloped to my car and drove down the street to pick up Beth. She brought her portable cassette player and we cranked the radio up to an ear-piercing decibel. Pearl Jam's "Alive" blared from the speakers. We swayed our heads from side to side and our long, straight manes covered our faces like we were Seattle grunge chicks.

I drove down Broadway, the main strip that cut through the middle of our small town. We felt liberated. The car had given us an inner strength that neither of us had experienced before. It was the empowerment of knowing we could go anywhere at any time. We wanted to yell to everybody in the street. We wanted to be punks.

As we approached the Broadway/Pulaski intersection, the light ahead turned red. I took my foot off the accelerator and placed it gingerly on the brake. There was just one problem - the car didn't slow. I stomped on the pedal until it hit the floor. The Corona jerked forward and stopped hard. Then it began to roll and the engine revved angrily. It was like it had a mind of its own and it decided to keep moving.

Beth grew concerned. "What's wrong?"

"I don't know. I've got the brake pushed all the way down."

"Why is it making that sound? Oh my God! It's going to explode." She tugged at the door handle, ready to bail out with a drop and roll.

"Don't leave me here!" I was rolling closer to the bumper in front of me. "What should I do?"

Beth though for a second. "I know. Put it in park!"

I pulled up on the emergency brake to slow us down some more, then shifted the car into park. It came to a sudden halt, whipping us forward. I almost bounced my head off the steering wheel and Beth fell into the dashboard. The engine revved louder.

"Okay, we're stopped," I said proudly, as if I'd saved our lives. Then the light turned green and the car behind us honked. It startled us and we jumped in our seats. I rambled, "What do we do, what do we do, what do we do…?"

The Cost of Living

Beth tried to act calm. "Okay, we know the car goes and we're only a few blocks from school. If we have to stop we either shift into park again or we can run it into a pole."

"Okay. Good plan."

I shifted back into drive and the car lurched forward. I made a sharp right and the high school was in sight. Unfortunately, the light ahead of us was turning yellow and I feared going through the same hell we had just experienced.

"Hold on," I yelled. Beth placed her palms upright on the roof of the car, as if we were going to roll over.

I floored the piece-of-shit Corona into the opposite lane, weaving in and out of cars. I cut across someone's lawn and ran over the curb into the school's parking lot. I pulled the emergency brake, skidded to about five miles an hour, and shifted into park. The engine began to rev even louder. I turned off the ignition, but the engine wouldn't die. It wouldn't even wheeze. The light brown, rusted, 1972 Toyota Corona with the gray spots was possessed. Beth and I ran from the car and into the school. We watched from the doorway, thinking it was going to blow sky high, but after five or so minutes the engine finally gave out, puttering in the end.

"The car wouldn't stop!" I yelled into the phone just outside the cafeteria. I had called Jean at work after my first class.

"What do you mean it wouldn't stop?" This was the fifth time she asked this question of me.

"Stop saying that! What do you think it means? It wouldn't stop!"

"What do you mean it wouldn't stop?"

I screamed, really screamed, like a lunatic. The car wouldn't stop driving, and Jean wouldn't stop driving me crazy. Then the bell rang. "I gotta go. I'm late for Physics. I'm leaving the car here for the night."

"Did you lock it up?"

Here I was, almost dead from Cujo the Corona, and my mother was worried about the possessed, demonic car being stolen.

That night, Jean called "The Guy" and told him what had happened. I begged her to take the car to a real mechanic, but she insisted that she had already paid for the work, so it should be performed to her satisfaction. "The Guy" came back sporadically for another two weeks. He told us that the accelerator had gotten stuck, but it wasn't his fault. After investigating the pedal on my own, I thought for sure that I smelled dried beer on it.

After fine-tuning the faulty accelerator, "The Guy" stated emphatically that the Corona was ready for the open road once again.

He was wrong.

The Cost of Living

To Beth's credit, she bravely entered the death-chariot and we cruised into Northport, a quaint fishing village along the Long Island Sound, to view the sunset. The problem on this go-around was the exact opposite of before. Each time I decelerated under ten miles per hour, the car stalled. As I approached traffic lights I had to gauge it just so, in order to keep the speedometer needle above ten while giving vehicles ahead of me ample time to go. At least we didn't have to contemplate smashing into anything to keep the car from moving, so we were finding the whole situation rather humorous.

After watching the sun fall and the orange glow of the sky fade, we bought ice cream at an old-fashioned parlor and returned to the car. I turned the ignition key and it wouldn't start. The Corona apparently felt it had done enough work for the day. Like the sun, it wasn't giving off anymore heat, which made me think that maybe it was solar-powered.

We sat on the curb waiting for a tow truck to arrive. Beth bought a pack of cigarettes, which we chain-smoked just to keep busy. Hours passed, along with several scores of "Rock-Paper-Scissors." Then, in the light emitted from the storefronts along Main Street, I saw a station wagon pull up and it looked awfully familiar. I stood up and squinted to make sure what I was seeing was real. From out of the car came a woman dressed in torn rags, wearing a dirtied scarf on her head and sneakers with holes. She hustled into a store that bore the sign "Good Will." I ran to the station wagon and checked the license plate. Sure enough, it was Jean.

My mother had donned the disguise of a needy woman in order to bargain-shop in the lowest priced store in town. I was mortified, and not because I thought people might mistakenly label us poor. This was a place for those less fortunate than us to shop for merchandise that they couldn't normally afford in retail stores. And here was my mother, going to a store for the needy because the prices were better.

I wanted to bust into the store and confront her, perhaps pull off her disguise and reveal the real Jean Kurchowski. I could hear the store manager question her as the sheriff applied the handcuffs, "Did you really think you could get away with buying our pasta maker for three dollars?"

"I would have," she'd say, like in Scooby-Doo, "if it wasn't for my meddling kid."

I peered through the window, watching my mother comb the aisles; but then Beth waved to me from across the street. "C.C.! Come on!" The tow truck had arrived, but I didn't want to give up this opportunity.

"Tell him to wait a minute!"

I discreetly entered the store, picking up my mother's trail. I spied on her from around corner shelves, waiting patiently for her to choose something so I could boldly unmask her. Finally she lifted a rectangular carton from the floor, and I prepared to swoop in for the kill. Then I noticed what she was buying.

The Cost of Living

My mother had picked up a car stereo, and I was sure it was for me. This was a serious conflict. How could I not allow her the pleasure of making the purchase and getting a great deal? I decided to humiliate her when we both got home.

The tow truck driver delivered me, Beth and the corroded Corona home. He explained that the car needed a lot more work and offered to take it to his garage. I knew Jean would just be mad and then force me to tow the car back to our house so "The Guy" could fix it again. I saved myself the money and the argument.

When Jean returned home, she ran upstairs with the car stereo I was not supposed to know she'd bought. During dinner I told her the story of the stalling and the tow truck and the latest update on the car's condition. She stomped to the phone to call "The Guy" but I interceded, begging her to let me get rid of it or to at least trade it in for a casket with wheels, which I deemed to be the same thing. She actually heard me this time, because she paused and hung up the phone. She thought for a moment and then came to a decision.

"Tell you what, it's time for me to get a new car. You can have my station wagon and we'll try to sell the brown thing-a-mabob."

I smiled. "Thank you," I said, with no small hint of relief.

Jean placed a three-line ad in the Pennysaver newspaper. It read: "Toyota Corona, body sound, engine runs, good second car." We received one response. He was a tubby, nerdy fellow in his late twenties who obviously didn't make a lot of money. I felt bad that we were pushing this tin-can on him, but Jean said it was up to him to purchase the car or walk away. I couldn't bring myself to go for the test drive and feigned a stomach ache. When Jean returned, she informed me that the car hadn't stalled once, as if questioning my honesty. The man asked what we wanted for the car. Jean blurted, "One thousand dollars." He mulled it over and offered $900. Jean acted as if she was being tortured for accepting such a low amount. Her profit: $125.

The next Saturday, I was shoveling the winter's first snowfall and heard honking from down the street. A large, family sized mini-van was heading my way. It was an odd color purple. By the looks of it, I thought it was a promotional set-up for the circus. When it pulled into our driveway I realized it was Jean's new car, and it was uglier than the Corona. Jean had stepped up from a station wagon to a mini-van, and it only meant she was going to be able to carry home more junk.

— Chapter Ten —
THE COST OF GOING AWAY TO COLLEGE

I was quite intimidated the first semester of my freshman year. A couple of weeks before the drive upstate from my home in good old, reliable Huntington to the unexplored, uncertain campus grounds of Ithaca, I panicked and let my fear get the best of me. I began asking myself many questions. Will my roommates like me? Will I like my roommates? This got me self-analyzing why I questioned my roommates liking me first, instead of vice-versa; which, naturally, sent me off on the whole tangent, "Am I meek?"

What if I wasn't ready to be kicked from the nest? What if my wings weren't strong enough to fly? Well, whatever paranoia I had prior to my first day of college, it subsided the day Jean drove me up for orientation.

Knowing she had me in a speeding car for five hours, and that I could do nothing without jeopardizing my life, Jean gave me suggestions, solely for my benefit, on how I could correct various aspects of my life. These included but were not limited to: my hair, my clothes, my study habits, my social life, hanging out with those greasy losers "who probably do pot," the food I eat, the glasses I wear, the books I read, the movies I watch, the music I listen to, my posture, my grammar, a poem I wrote in the third grade, my love life, my toothbrush, how not to be a breach baby next time, my penmanship, my ability to accept criticism, my tone, my language, my respect for my mother and all that she's done for me, my capacity to "listen," my understanding of the difference between "critical" and "helpful", and, of course, my attitude!

By the time I arrived at school, I was so angry that I simply tossed my suitcases from the back of her van to the curb and screamed at her to go home immediately. By the time I got to my room, I was sobbing. Lisa Cantrell, a lovely, carefree brunette from the small berg of Cherry Grove up near Buffalo, was the lucky soul assigned as my roommate. I could only imagine this young woman opening the door and seeing this pathetic, weeping sack of flesh stretched across the floor.

The Cost of Living

Luckily, Lisa comforted me. Through my quivering lip I was able to make out the words that described the 5-hour berating I had just received from my mother. Lisa's solution to my problem was to get drunk. Actually, that was Lisa's solution to every problem, which might be why Lisa failed out the first semester.

It didn't matter, though. She made perfect sense at the time.

Although never officially declared, my minor in raucous fun had officially commenced. I made sure to get good grades except for the occasional B-minus, but I certainly didn't let studying get in the way of a good time. I dated many boys and even had sex with a few. As sick as it may sound, there were times I imagined Jean during some of those sessions. Right in the throes of something resembling passion, my mother's scowl would appear on the ceiling, admonishing me. The pleasure I received from this vengeance lasted longer than the men I was with.

By the time Christmas break arrived, I was falling into a routine and feeling more comfortable with myself. The bed hopping had come to a halt and solid relationships were being forged. The sad thing was that I still held a grudge against Jean. I rarely called her, and when I did I pretty much grunted through the short conversation. I sensed her growing concern, and by the tone of her voice I knew she was going to explode when I returned for the holidays... so I plunged the knife

119

deeper and didn't give her the opportunity. The day before my bus ride home, I called Jean to inform her that my plans had changed. I was going to spend Christmas in Florida, with my father. Double whammy!

Late that night, a few friends and I were throwing Lisa a going-away party. Unwilling to prostitute herself to her professors and without enough money for any serious bribes, her grades were not strong enough to get her invited back in January, so Lisa didn't even bother taking her final exams. Instead, she partied like a sailor on leave since she knew her immediate destiny was to slave in her father's Hyundai showroom.

It was a small gathering in our room with the two girls next door, Jen and Jo, and a couple of boys, Billy Woods and Howie Rosen. While passing a joint around with a couple of liters of beer, we heard a commotion just outside the door. My roommate turned the music down to listen.

"CAROLINE!"

I had heard my name being called like that a million times before; it was becoming my worst nightmare. I shut my eyes and hoped it would go away. My friends froze. We heard the dorm director's voice from down the corridor.

"Maam! Please!"

"CAROLINE!"

The Cost of Living

Jean reached the door and jiggled the knob. "Caroline! Are you in there?" The dorm director pleaded with her to be quiet.

"My daughter's in there! Open this door."

My friends scattered to perform their respective pot-camouflage duties: Spraying Lysol, shaking baby powder into the air, lighting incense. I just stared at the door, trying to keep it shut with my eyes, the type of thing you believe you can do when you're stoned. Unfortunately, it doesn't work in Realtown, USA. With a good running start and a shoulder unusually muscular for a woman, Jean knocked the door in.

She was wearing sweats under her parka and her head had steam rising off of it as she perspired. As she panted desperately to catch her breath, I had a humorous vision of her running down the highway, not driving. I giggled, which should not be construed as a good thing.

"Caroline!"

I furrowed my brow. "What are you doing here?"

"Do you have to have an abortion?"

Billy Woods, a kid I'd had sex with just the previous night, gasped. Typical of a boy this age, he thought it was possible to know that quickly. Jean glared at him. I think she might have even snorted at him.

I stood up to confront my accuser. "What the hell are you talking about? I'm not pregnant. If I was pregnant, wouldn't I have told you?"

Billy Woods high-fived Howie Rosen. "Aw-right!"

"Then why aren't you coming home for Christmas?" she asked.

"Because I'm sick of you. I hate you right now!"

It felt so good to scream, except that my mouth was dry and I could really have gone for a Snickers. Or, better yet, a chocolate milk shake. No, no! Pudding!

"So you're not having an abortion, then?"

I laughed at the insanity of this question. "No."

"Fine. Have a Merry Christmas. Leave an address on my answering machine so I know where to send your presents."

Jean raced out of the room and down the hall. I chased after her. "Mom!" She turned to face me. We were only about ten feet apart from each other, but emotionally it was much farther. We didn't really have anything to say to each other. Jean knew why I was mad at her and why I acted the way I did, but she was never one to say she was sorry. This little drama was her way of saying she cared. My mother had driven five hours in the cold night to make sure I was all right and that I had someone there for me if I was in trouble. I decided right then that I was going to be there for her.

"I'll see you tomorrow," I said. She nodded and placed the hood of her parka over her head. Her face disappeared into the fur and I wanted to laugh, but was able to control myself. By then, everybody who lived in the residence hall had come out to watch my mother leave. She hopped in her minivan and drove up the hill toward the highway.

The Cost of Living

After being written up for breaking dorm rules and destroying dorm property, my friends and I went back to our celebration. An hour later I sighed, thinking I could have gone back with Jean instead of on a slow bus the next morning. Then I realized that she must have thought of that, too. Jean couldn't take a crap without thinking of thirty different ways to do it. She probably understood what would have happened if we'd spent another five hours in the car together, so she never suggested it. I'd like to think it was one of her Christmas presents to me, the only one that didn't come from a garage sale.

— Chapter Eleven —

THE COST OF THANKSGIVING DINNER

It was Thanksgiving break and I was about to spend my entire holiday with strangers who seemed stranger by the minute. Following the little drama in my dorm room the previous year, Jean had come to the conclusion that she needed new friends. She'd researched several singles' publications and found a few local groups that she could meet with a couple of nights a week.

The one she'd chosen to attend was for single men and women in their forties and fifties. The social gatherings were conducted at the high school library, which seemed apropos since the twenty-some-odd members split off into cliques and gossiped about each other much like the high school teenagers

I'd left behind after graduation. In addition to weekly bitch sessions, they planned an outing once a month to a museum, a Broadway show or a beach barbecue. For months Jean had begged me to join her on one of these trips to meet her friends, but I just didn't believe it was necessary. I couldn't imagine any young adult who wanted to accompany their mother to her friends' party.

Sometimes I sensed that Jean merely wanted to prove that she wasn't alone in the world, that she did in fact have family; but I felt it was in her best interest that I cut the apron strings and let her find her own way - not to mention, it sounded like one big bore.

From time to time Jean pushed herself to socialize, but it rarely lasted long. The bowling league or volunteer work at the hospital, the kennel, and the soup kitchen usually ended with the realization that there were no freebies to take home. Had there been a shopping club, my mother would have been President for Life, but shopping is an individual sport. Besides, nobody could ever manage to maintain the same stamina in a shopping mall that it had taken Jean years to build. Nor would most people want to.

Much to my surprise, Jean did maintain this new circle of friends for some time. She continued to invite them over to the house for backyard parties. I couldn't understand how she could proudly answer the door and let people in with the house in shambles. There was no place to sit since the couches and chairs were covered with papers and knickknacks; the rugs and floors hadn't been washed in years, and the kitchen emitted a scent that couldn't have been identified by NASA scientists. It was as if she was blind to the way she lived. I, on the other hand, was completely humiliated and made it a point to never be home when my mother entertained.

Unfortunately, I was unaware of her Thanksgiving plans until I returned from college the day before the feast. Upon walking through the door, I saw a Jean I had never seen before. She was busy shoving items in drawers and closets to clear space. This behavior was a close relative to cleaning, so it pleased me.

"C.C., thank God you're back. Give me a hand and find the table extensions," she said as she moved between rooms.

"What table extensions?"

"The extensions. For the table," she put forth with that lilt in her voice that implied I needed to start thinking for myself.

"That doesn't help me. By asking 'what table extensions' I'm really asking, 'We have table extensions?'" I took off my coat and began unloading clothes from my suitcase into the washing machine.

"Washer's broken. It doesn't rinse all the way. You just have to pour four pitchers of water on top of the clothes. No more than four. I've almost figured out how to fix it," she said, still frantically throwing this and that into there and those.

"The table extensions. They came with the table. It was a good deal."

"Mom, we've never used table extensions." I was becoming increasingly curious as to what they looked like and where they could possibly be, until it dawned on me. "Why do we need table extensions?"

"For the guests. We're having guests this year. Isn't that nice?"

"Grandma?" That was my only guess. After that I couldn't fathom who might be coming to the Kurchowski house for Thanksgiving.

Jean chuckled, "Wouldn't that be something?"

I suddenly felt a little strange inside. A shiver went up my spine and through my brain, causing me to sweat - similar to the time Jean had forced me to sneak into the movie theater. Something felt very "off". I looked around, not for table extensions, but to notice what there wasn't to notice. I had seen this investigative strategy in television shows and movies. A lot of preparation goes into making a Thanksgiving feast and Jean's kitchen was pretty bare of the typical trimmings for such a meal. There was no turkey, no cranberries, no potatoes, no stuffing. A thought crossed my mind that elicited a loud giggle.

"Did I miss something?" she asked.

"No. It's just that for a moment I thought you might be catering this dinner, and then I realized how much that would cost... Forget it. Are you planning on getting up really early tomorrow morning?"

"It's a pot luck. Everybody's bringing something."

"Mom? Who's everybody?" I pretty much already knew this answer.

"My friends. This is the party house. They come here all the time. Nobody had anywhere to go this year, so we're having dinner together. Isn't that nice?"

"None of them have families or kids of their own?" I was not looking forward to spending the holiday with a bunch of unfamiliar stragglers.

"We've become like family," Jean said.

"We've? You mean we've, as in you and me have become like their family? Or we've like you and they have become like family?" I'm not sure why I needed this clarification, but suddenly I felt as though I was being shoved out of the inner circle that had previously only included my mother and me.

"We've. Me and my friends. We've." More and more I was becoming a visitor.

Still, I looked all over for the mysterious table extensions. The usual spots like closets, the basement, the garage and under the beds proved fruitless. There was a time when I was a little girl and I could still hide inside or underneath some of these places, but now they were havens for junk - and not just Jean's junk, but other people's junk as well. If there was a sign posted to a telephone pole announcing in black magic marker "Garage

Sale", Jean was stopping. If there was a mug that was barely chipped, a shirt that was barely stained, a book that was barely torn, a game that was barely played, a bike that was barely ridden, or a chair that was barely broken, more than likely it could be found stored somewhere in this house. In my mother's eyes, "barely" is a very broad term.

Truly believing that whatever table extensions might have existed were forever lost in this abyss, I instead opened a can of soda, absentmindedly checking the expiration date first, and focused my efforts on cleaning the kitchen. The mail had piled up on the table, the dishes had piled up in the sink, and grease had piled up on the stove. While Jean was pouring pitchers of water on my clothes I sorted the junk mail on the table. Then I yelled to Jean, "What do you want me to do with the mail?"

"There's a box on the dining room table, throw it in there. I'll bring it up to my bed and sort it later!" I did as instructed and then moved to the counters, throwing out expired cans and bottles. A small, store-bought yellow cake with chocolate icing was sitting out. The lid's cellophane was ripped open. The expiration date told me it was three months past its prime and my finger told me it was starting to stale. I tossed it in. "Should I just throw the food on the counter into the cupboards?"

"Bring it to the basement for me," she yelled from the laundry room.

I ditched outside and heaved the bag into the pail. I yelled goodnight as I resigned to my room, a ten-by-ten foot sanctuary that still bore relics of a past teenage life. Or so I thought.

Upon opening the door, I quickly found that my room was no longer C.C.'s room. It was the new room for storage. Jean was running out of space. There were cardboard boxes stacked everywhere with the sole exception of the bed. She may have taken over my room, but at least she'd left me a place to sleep.

Knowing that the sheets hadn't been changed or washed by pitcher since the day I had last been there, I stripped the bed and pulled a clean set of sheets from my bag. After making up the bed, I crashed for the night.

The next morning was spent vacuuming, dusting and scraping as I tried to get nearly fifteen years of muck off the floors and walls to make the house presentable. I actually believe it meant more to me than it did to Jean, who continued moving objects around to make the place seem more like a home owned by a collector rather than Fred Sanford's illegitimate child.

By noon I was mopping the linoleum floor with hopes of removing the brown layer from the top and returning it to its original cream coloring, when the doorbell rang announcing that the first guest had arrived.

One by one I met Jean's friends as they made their entrance, each carrying their own contribution to the dinner. First there was Gerald, a balding man whose three rubbery chins swung side to side as he shuffled, his feet turned outward due to his thighs chafing together, carrying a pot of sweet potatoes. After an awkward introduction that included shaking a clammy hand, Gerald excused himself to take a look at the broken washer for Jean. Gerald was not a plumber, but apparently he could fix anything. At least that's what Jean claimed. More than likely he mentioned turning on a faucet once, so Jean considered him a master plumber who could repair pipes. For free. Jean would claim Jeffrey Dahmer was a great babysitter if he was willing to watch the kids for free.

Next through the door came the stuffing made by Sheila, a meek woman with teased black hair and a throaty voice whose tongue always seemed to be hanging from her open mouth. Not five minutes later Bob followed with more sweet potatoes. Bob was a twitchy guy with a long face and eyes as big as golf balls, who was always blinking hard as if he was trying to extract a small pebble from beneath the lid. Bringing the cranberries was Sandy, a broad, solid woman with puffed up hair pushed so far in front of her face that I truly believed she was returning from her class in clown college and had forgotten to take off the wig.

Finally there was Larry, a six-foot, three-inch lanky fellow whose facial features - nose, chin, mustache, and hairline - all seemed to come to a point. Sadly, Larry's teeth were pointy as well, making him look like an unusually tall rodent. Larry was the only male guest not to bring sweet potatoes. He'd brought white mashed.

The Cost of Living

Most unfortunate was the fact that no one had bothered to bring a bird. It seemed Jean's invitation to dinner was much more for her to seem like a generous hostess while at the same time receiving a free dinner. It was genius! What Jean didn't understand was that her guests had sort of expected that she would cook the turkey while they supplied the side dishes.

"Why would anybody expect that?" Jean asked me while we frantically searched for something that would be an equal substitute for a Thanksgiving entree. The kitchen refrigerator was full of pizza and fast-food leftovers along with lots of salad dressings, condiments and assorted beverages. The basement refrigerator contained more bulk items, such as boxes of hamburgers, boxes of frankfurters, crates of spoiling fruit, and more assorted beverages. The freezer in the garage, however, had a shelf dedicated to frozen fried chicken that several years ago had been cleared off a supermarket shelf during a three-for-one sale.

So, after cooking up the fried chicken, the seven of us gathered around the table that, minus extensions, only seated four. Gerald's girth, while it might not have hindered working on the washing machine, made it tougher to fit around the feast. I was literally pressed against other people throughout the entire meal. Elbows were knocking me in the ribs and my glass was knocked into my teeth each time I tried to drink. Trying to use a fork and knife with my arms pinned to my sides was so difficult that I dreamed about how much easier it would be to just throw my face into my plate and chow down.

The conversation around the table was much like the dinner, quick and cheap. There were no discussions of politics or pop culture. It was more like short snippets one might hear at an old folks' home. 'Complaining about ailments' edged out 'complaining about people' as the topic of choice, but only by a little.

"Uck! The veins in my legs keep getting bluer," Sheila divulged. "If I dye my hair the same color, I might get away with it."

Bob's eyelids batted away. "Don't leave your things unattended at the Y. I hear they steal."

"Do you know what Gretchen said Rita said about me?" Sandy whispered loudly, leaning in to tell her secret. "I'm two-faced. That bitch! Now I have to act nice when we go to the theater."

Gerald picked his teeth, surveying the food. "Is anybody going to finish those last two pieces of chicken?"

Larry excused himself to go to the bathroom. The remaining guests looked at each other, rolling their eyes as if to say, "Uh-oh!"

Once Larry was out of earshot, I felt compelled to inquire.

"What's wrong?"

Sheila went first, her voice so raspy you'd swear she'd just inhaled a carton of cigarettes. "The man smells."

I was ill-prepared for her bluntness.

"Like a sewage plant," Sandy added.

"Somebody should tell him," suggested Bob.

"I wouldn't want to know," Gerald said. "Is everyone done with the potatoes?" I passed him all three dishes and, without conscience for how his gluttony appeared to others, he loudly clanged the spoon against his plate to release the clumped potatoes. I wished I could be that complacent with ignorance.

"Maybe I should just bring out the dessert," Jean offered, and she scampered into the kitchen.

"Fabulous," Gerald said as potatoes fell from his mouth. It made me sick and I looked around the table for someone to help me acknowledge his appalling eating habits, but no one else really cared. They were either used to it or they accepted him for who he was. Was I wrong to pass judgment? I looked back to Gerald who was desperately trying to lick a little potato that had escaped to his upper lip. No, I wasn't wrong.

I looked around at these misfits and thought about how I really did not want to spend another holiday with these people. Yet, at the same time, I felt reassured that my mother had a life that was not just about shopping and me. Maybe these new friends would help her develop better social skills and teach her that there is more to life than bargain hunting and penny pinching, which is when it occurred to me…

"What dessert?" I thought.

My eyes went as wide as Bob's golf balls when I realized that last night's garbage cake was supposed to be tonight's dessert. I excused myself, squeezing out of the human wedge I was caught in, and ran to the kitchen.

"Mom, I'm sorry, but I threw…"

My voice trailed off the moment I saw it. The cake was on a plate. Jean was cutting it into little squares. I scrutinized it first, so I wouldn't accuse Jean unfairly. Yes, it was a flat yellow cake with chocolate icing. Yes, there was a box sitting next to it. Yes, the cellophane window on top of the box was ripped loose; and yes, it had to be the same cake that I had dumped in the garbage the previous night.

"The cake…"

"What about it?" She asked this so innocently that I actually answered in a way that made it seem like she truly had no idea what this conversation was going to be about.

"I threw out a cake just like this last night," I explained with an exasperated cough, to emphasize how she wasn't going to talk her away out of this one.

"Oh, I know. Thank you," she said ever so sincerely.

"Then why did you pull it out of the trash?"

"I didn't. This is another one I had in the fridge."

"But, but…" I was trying so hard to keep my composure and maintain a clear line of events in my head: There was a cake, chocolate frosting, ripped cellophane, in the garbage last night, on the counter today… "You pulled that out of the garbage!"

136

"C.C., would I serve my guests dessert that had been in the garbage?"

My head shook violently with the realization. "Oh, my God. Yes. Yes, you would."

She scoffed as she picked up the plate and brought it into the dining room. I was so disgusted, I thought I might vomit. What had she become? I rushed to the threshold of the dining room to watch. As morbid as it was, I just had to look and be sure that when I went into therapy I could tell my psychiatrist that this really had happened.

"Jean, did you make that?" Sheila asked.

"Looks tasty," Gerald said.

As she dished out the squares of garbage cake, something miraculous happened. Before any of them could take a bite, a loud, echoed moaning sound emanated from the ceiling. All eyes looked up.

Then we heard the bathroom door open and Larry emerged. These people didn't lie. The odor that came from that room could have killed a cow. Larry, apparently oblivious to his own gases, pointed back to the bathroom and asked, "Jean, is there something wrong with your plumbing? I tried flushing and flushing..."

Suddenly another loud moan came from the ceiling. Then Gerard, trying to remember what he'd done when he was fixing the washer, said, "I connected that pipe to that pipe..."

And then it appeared - a water stain forming in the middle of the ceiling, directly above us, quickly grew to a massive stain. Then the stain began to drip. Everybody pushed back from the table just in time. Within seconds, WOOSH! The ceiling collapsed and water cascaded on top of the table, flooding the now empty dishes and soaking the garbage cake. With a lack of support to hold them up in the attic above, BAM! a pair of two-by-five boards crashed down next, smashing the garbage cake for good, just in case anyone (Gerald) still thought it might be edible.

"My table extensions!" Jean exclaimed. Then she placed her hands on her hips and stated with proud wonderment, "Would you look at that!"

— Chapter Twelve —

THE COST OF
GOOD HEALTH

Something inside my head was screaming, "You should have known." Of course, in hindsight there were many clues: The choking up in her voice when she called, which she'd claimed was just a sore throat; the letters I started receiving on a more than daily basis; her sudden curiosity in my religious beliefs; the questions regarding her will. But again, that's just in hindsight.

It was odd for me to contemplate the mortality of my parents. I didn't think I'd ever hear that my father, with Blowjob Betty down in Florida, was dead. Oh, I knew someday it was inevitable that he'd die; I would just never hear about it, unless of course it was due to some bar fight in which he was brutally murdered and it made the news.

My mother, I'd always figured, would outlive me. She was going to be around to whisper in my ear and critique my life, especially my spending habits, providing me with twenty or so options for any given situation, whether asked for or not. And when it would come time to bury me, I imagined my mother telling the funeral director that cardboard is just as good as wood, and digging a grave should only cost $23, less if the soil is unusually soft that day.

Now I was faced with the unthinkable. On the day I finished my "final" final exam, I returned to my dorm to grab my stuff and drive back home for the summer. The phone rang just as I stepped across the threshold. It was Jean.

"Hi, sweetie! It's me. How'd ya do?"
"Fine. No problem, I think."
"Good, good. Listen, honey, I have cancer."

That's how she told me. She just blurted it out, matter-of-factly. More precisely it turned out to be breast cancer, which was ironic since for such a heavy-set woman, she practically had no breasts. I think Jean wore a Double-A bra, in fact. Cancer cells must be female, because they show no preference for breast size.

The Cost of Living

As tears welled up in my eyes, I asked her when she'd found out. "Oh, a couple of weeks ago," she stated nonchalantly. A couple of weeks ago? And she hadn't told me? "I didn't want to worry you," was her explanation.

Furious, I hung up the telephone, jumped in my car, and sped back home. The entire trip I tried to figure out and understand why she hadn't told me sooner. How could she not tell me? Better yet, how dare she!

At first it seemed logical that she'd waited to tell me. She didn't want my concern for her to affect my exams. But then I realized that she told me immediately before I set out on my five-hour trip through snaking mountains on treacherous roads. My life can be at risk, but God forbid my grades should suffer. "My little Caroline. She crashed in a flaming wreck, but at least she made Dean's List."

By the time I got home, the sun had already set. The eggplant-hued minivan was in the driveway. Leaving my things in the car, I raced into the house. Jean was watching "Jeopardy." I stopped at the entryway to the den. My first instinct was to yell at her for not letting me be there for her. Luckily, my second instinct took over. I plopped down beside her and threw my arms around her. I held her tight, crying. No words needed to be spoken. My mother was very sick.

She was to be operated on in two days. As it turned out, this wasn't the first time she'd had a tumor in her breast. When I was three, she'd had a lumpectomy performed. Now that a second tumor had been found, she had no choice but to lose the breast.

The following day I drove Jean to the hospital and helped her at the admissions desk. Her room was shared with a frail woman in her eighties, but in spite of physical weakness she was emotionally vibrant and talkative. After speaking with this roommate for only thirty minutes, I knew she was the kind of Grandmother I had always wanted. She asked my mother what she was in for and the two began discussing their ailments. The elderly woman, Victoria, had diverticulitis.

"Oh, that's a good one!" Jean exclaimed. "Everybody gets cancer, but to say you survived diverticulitis… well! Now that's a story. I mean, who wants to hear about a bad boob that's about to be lopped off, right?"

This was an obvious cue to talk about the cancer. Thankfully, Victoria was a solid listener who seemed genuinely concerned yet optimistic. She was a very comforting woman and I felt relieved that there was someone in the very next bed whom I could consult to ensure my mother was receiving proper treatment. When Victoria left to go for a stroll down the hallway, the room felt a bit emptier and less cheerful. It got worse when Jean yelled, "What a nosy old biddy! Does she ever shut up?"

The Cost of Living

I unloaded my mother's magazines and crossword puzzles, making certain she was as settled as possible before visiting hours ended. That night, as I slept in the emptiness of her house, I thought about our years together. Jean was my only family. Except for mean, old Grandma and Daddy Dude in Fort Lauderdale, she was all I had.

I couldn't sleep a wink. I strolled around the disaster-zone my mother called home, the house I'd been raised in, seeing the garbage with more nostalgic eyes. I studied the portraits on the wall, tracing my lineage. I couldn't get over how beautiful my mother had been at my age. She still kept her wedding picture hanging in the hallway, a testament to the fact that a man had indeed desired her enough to marry her. I thought about the family that might have been.

Snooping through her closets, I found some old shoe boxes of photo albums that Jean had stored. There were pictures of her and me in the Catskills when I was a baby; yellowed Kodak shots of me in various Halloween costumes through the years. I had been a Gnu, Howard the Duck, Michael Dukakis, Gloria Swanson - the list goes on. Their lone common denominator: They had all been bought in the "99¢ or less" rack. None of these guises were what I'd wanted, but Jean had instilled in me the little ditty, "It doesn't matter who you be, as long as all the candy's free."

I watched television until the sun came up, took a shower, and went to the kitchen to make myself breakfast. I peered in the refrigerator and quickly lost my appetite. The shelves were filled with moldy bread and layers upon layers of tupperware. There was green stuff in plastic containers, blue stuff in plastic containers, and black stuff in plastic containers. Frankly, I was in the mood for yellow and brown stuff, so I headed to the diner in town and forced down a couple of eggs and a bagel. I decided that once I heard from the doctor that the operation had been successful, I would clean out the refrigerator along with some other neglected areas of the house.

When I arrived at the hospital before the surgery that morning, my mother had already been injected with an anesthetic. She lay helpless on a gurney, too weak to hold her eyelids open. At first I thought she was asleep, but she started muttering incoherently. I held her hand.

She whispered, "Caroline?"

"I'm here, Mom," I reassured her.

"Listen, honey..."

"Don't try to talk, Mom." Why ruin the moment, I thought.

"No. I have to tell you this. If I should die..."

"You're not going to die, Mom." It wasn't just hope that made me say these words. I was sure of it now, that she would come through this.

"But if I do, you have to promise me something."

"What?"

"Promise me you won't throw out anything in the house."

I laughed at the irony since that was my very plan.

"First thing I'm going to do is throw everything out." I didn't feel bad, joking like that. I figured that if I didn't add some levity to the situation, Jean would think she was in worse shape than she actually was.

"No! Don't!" Her voice was raised as if her life depended on me hearing this vital instruction. She didn't have the strength to open her eyes, but she mustered enough to make me listen.

"Why not?"

"There's money everywhere!" She had to be kidding. I'd spent the previous night reminiscing through every room, and hadn't come across a penny.

"Where is there money?"

Sounding like Marlon Brando in the Godfather, she struggled to say, "The cotton balls. There's money in the cotton balls."

And then two orderlies entered and wheeled Jean away.

It's probably a bit morbid to think it, and downright disturbing to admit it, but as I sat in the lobby waiting to hear from the doctor, all I could think about was the damn cotton balls. How much money was she talking about? Tens? Hundreds? Thousands? Is she crazy? Of course she's crazy, Caroline, she's your mother.

I started obsessing about the damn cotton balls. I knew that the moment I walked through her front door again I was going to check the cotton balls. If there was in fact money there, I would be searching that house from top to bottom. I told myself that when I uncovered her bounty I would hide it, merely to illustrate to my mother the logic of keeping money in a bank.

An hour and a half after wheeling my mother into surgery, Dr. Granato appeared to give me the news. He told me everything had gone as well as could be expected, and he anticipated a full recovery. I was grateful that the surgery had gone well, but I was also grateful that the waiting was over, because now I could check the cotton balls.

I dashed out to my car and hustled home. I had about five hours before Jean would wake from her post-operative sleep, expecting me to be sitting diligently by her side.

I was sitting on the floor of Jean's bathroom, digging deep into the generic-brand artifacts beneath her sink, trying to find the damn cotton balls. Hundreds of items packed the cabinet. Most of it was from the time that she'd wanted to be an Avon Lady. She'd never sold anything; she just kept the free samples - which, it had just occurred to me, was the only reason she'd became an Avon Lady in the first place, her tenure having lasted exactly twelve days.

Finally I came across a yellowed box against the wall in the back. The date on the box read "September 17, 1979." I buried my hand deep into the cotton and hit the bottom. When I pulled out my hand, I found myself clutching a wad of fifties totaling three thousand dollars.

The next four hours were spent hunting for the rest of Jean's loot. I found five hundred dollars in an old pillow, a little over a thousand stuffed in a plastic soda bottle underneath the kitchen sink, and about eighteen hundred taped to the underside of a dresser drawer. I knew I hadn't even scratched the surface, and decided to teach my mother a lesson.

I put the money in a large, manila envelope and drove down to the bank to open up a joint savings account in both our names. As I waited for the woman at the bank to finish typing up the paperwork, I grinned at the thought of Jean going ballistic, trying to remember where she'd put the money.

When I returned to the house, I put on a pair of yellow, latex cleaning gloves and went to work. Tackling the refrigerator was the first order of business. Anything that was not the color of normal food was tossed. I checked every date on all the bottles and packaging. I found a bottle of Russian dressing dated September of 1979 and surmised that she'd bought it the same day as the cotton balls. It took two hours and six extra-strength garbage bags, but the refrigerator was free of all possible plague-inducing, spoiled food.

The next week was more of the same. I'd visit Jean in the hospital and then go back home to scrub some part of the house. I thought about attempting the garage, but she would have to come down with some malady that kept her bedridden a full month before I would be able to complete such a task.

The morning Jean was to be released, I admirably inspected the house before I picked her up and signed her out. I was giddy at the prospect of Jean returning to a tidy home. As I tenderly escorted her through the front door, she glanced around the foyer.

"Well, look what you did…"

"You like?"

"Nice, very nice."

She hobbled over to the kitchen while I brought her suitcase up to her bedroom. Just as I laid it down on her bed, she screamed up at me. "CAROLINE!"

I raced down the stairs, thinking she must have fallen. When I reached the kitchen, she was standing in front of the refrigerator with the door wide open.

"You threw out my food?!"

"I cleaned out your refrigerator for you."

"Where the hell is my tuna fish?"

"What?"

"My tuna fish. It was in a little container."

Tuna fish? In which of the fifty containers? "I did not see anything resembling tuna fish in there, unless tuna fish is a fuzzy forest green these days."

"Who asked you to clean out the refrigerator?" She was pissed.

"Nobody asked me. I was doing you a favor."

"By throwing out good food?"

"None of that food was good. It was unrecognizable. Some of the dates on the bottles were from the seventies!"

"You don't pay attention to the dates. They only put those on there because the government forces them to do it. Everybody knows that." She slammed the refrigerator door shut.

"Mom, it was all spoiled."

"You think I eat spoiled food? Am I dead yet?" She went into the den and fell down on the couch in a huff. No, she wasn't dead yet. She was close, but she'd survived…

I knew I shouldn't leave her, but my fury was building even though she was in a sickly state. I grabbed my jacket and walked out the door. I went for a long drive. I parked my car in my old high school parking lot and sat there to cool off. She was my mother, she was sick, and I needed to stay as calm as possible.

When I returned a little while later, the house looked like it had when she'd first gone into the hospital. In the short time I'd been gone, she'd managed to fill the sink with dishes, strew newspapers and magazines across the carpets, spill some juice on the sofa which she had yet to sop up, and clog the toilet. My anger was quickly returning.

Then I looked over to my mother, snoring on the couch next to a pile of gnawed off chicken bones. She was alive. She was relaxed. She was home. And after all, it was her home.

Oddly enough, this was the first time I remember feeling like an adult. I looked around and no longer saw myself in this house. I saw memories of a little girl who'd occupied this house, but it suddenly matched the personality of its owner, not me, a mere occupant. It wasn't a part of me, but it was all of Jean.

I sensed my freedom swiftly approaching. I would soon have my own home, decorated with a touch of elegance unabated by cost. It would be a place that reeked of respect and not a year-old meatloaf; but Jean could be comfortable here, even if no one else in their right mind could.

— Chapter Thirteen —
THE COST OF GOOD LANDSCAPING

I frantically jiggled my keys in the lock as I counted the rings from the telephone. For some odd reason, I sensed that this was an important call I did not want to miss. One of the bags of groceries I was carrying slipped from my arm and various pieces of fruit rolled down the stairs to the apartment below mine. A couple of apples hit against old Mr. Durbin's door. Thinking someone was knocking, he opened the door just in time for an orange to pass by him.

"Is this garbage?" he asked.

"Just a second, Mr. Durbin," I told him as I finally got the door open. Panting furiously, I threw the other bag to the couch and grabbed the receiver just as the machine picked up. An irritating squelch of interference erupted in my ear. I should have taken this as a sign and hung the phone up immediately. Instead, I made the mistake of saying, "Hello?"

"Caroline? Are you there?"

It was Beth. "Yes, I'm here. What's up?"

"The question is: What's up with your mother and those wood chips?"

Wood chips? I could have imagined a million different scenarios involving wood chips, if only I had known what "wood chips" really were. Was she covered in wood chips? Did the house become so decrepit that it had fallen into a pile of wood chips?

I raced back down the stairs, telling Mr. Durbin that the fruits were his to keep. He had already assumed as much, since he was waving goodbye with a half-eaten apple in his hand.

The entire drive over to Jean's house was filled with dread. What horrors and embarrassment had my mother tormented the neighborhood with now, thereby humiliating me in the process? As I hyperventilated and screamed at an elderly couple for not moving the nanosecond the light turned green at an intersection, I finally convinced myself that I was overreacting. Perhaps I was using my mother as a scapegoat to detract from insecurities I was currently feeling about myself.

I was already past a quarter of a century and had no serious relationship. I hadn't even dated in more than a month. Several times I'd picked up the phone to call Greg, just to pretend that I was still able to communicate with the opposite sex. Once I even waited for him to say 'hello' before hanging up. Lately I'd been perusing the personal ads, until I realized this was what my mother was doing. Jean still went on dates. In fact, I could tell she was actually engaged in sexual intercourse.

When Jean was going through periods of sexual drought, she was more critical than usual. She would find fault with not just material things like the décor in my living room, but with ideas. If, during one of these dry spells, I was to mention that I was thinking about vacationing in Florida, she would tell me I was making a huge mistake because they charge too much to rent a car down there.

However, Jean had been dating a lot at this time. She was downright peppy; she would do, do, do. I finally came to the conclusion that these wood chips were some sort of project for her. In the words of Jean, "See!? I was right!"

Before I even pulled up to the house, all the way from the far end of her street, I saw them. Or at least I saw a giant shape smack dab in the middle of her driveway. I didn't need to guess, since I knew what they had to be - they were wood chips, and they were piled higher than me.

I parked in front of the house, right behind her car, which could no longer fit in the driveway since the entire driveway surface, normally big enough to fit four cars and maybe several motorcycles, was covered over five feet high with wood chips. A shovel stood upright out of the top of the pile, as if soldiers had planted the flag at Iwo Jima.

Upon exiting my car, the first thing I did, completely out of habit, was look to see if anyone was watching. To this day I believe "The Neighborhood Watch" program was created with my mother in mind. Who could avoid staring at the spectacle of the crazy lady?

As I pondered the mountain of dead wood in front of me, Jean came around the corner from the backyard; she was pushing an empty wheelbarrow toward me, coming for the wood chips, no doubt. She waved with a big smile and lost control of the wheelbarrow, tipping it over. I ran over to help her.

"Are you out of your mind?" I asked rhetorically.

"Don't worry. It's not broken."

"Not the wheelbarrow! The chips! Where on earth did you get all these wood chips?" I never should have asked this question. I already knew the answer.

"They were free."

Of course, they were free. It was a dumb question.

She continued as she righted the wheelbarrow and headed toward the chips. "These guys were destroying trees down the street, you know, in one of those mulchers. I asked what they were doing with the chips, and they said they were going to dump them; so I told them to dump them here."

The Cost of Living

I couldn't fathom what anybody would do with all these chips. Usually people scattered them in specific areas, but there was enough in Jean's driveway to build a cabin. As Jean climbed to the top of the pile and shoveled chips into the wheelbarrow, I mistakenly asked, "What are you going to do with all these?"

"I'm going to put them around the yard."

"You'll kill the grass."

"The grass is already dead."

She was right. The grass was dead. Not completely, just patches of dead. Whatever grass still existed was thinning out like hair on a middle-aged man's head. The reason for the lack of lawn was obvious to everybody but Jean. On her small parcel of property, she had too many trees. The trees kept the sun from reaching the grass. Jean didn't accept this explanation, because if she did, it would mean she would have to cut the trees down. Tree cutting costs money.

In Jean's infinite wisdom, it made much more sense to layer the remaining strands of grass with free, minced trees.

"Grab a shovel and give me a hand," she said.

"No! I will not contribute to this lunacy! This is nuts! These are wood chips!"

I headed to my car in a huff. She was doing it again. All I could think was that the neighbors were probably mad at having to look at yet another eyesore at the Kurchowski house.

Two young teens on Schwinns pedaled by, laughing at the crazy lady atop the wood chips.

I looked back at her. They were laughing at my sixty-year old mother, breaking her back shoveling wood chips. This was her house. I tried to tell myself I should not contribute to her madness, but how could I leave her to do this hard work alone? I took a deep breath and returned to Mount Jean.

As I walked across the dirt that should be a lawn, I felt some strange movement beneath my feet. I stopped for a moment, my left foot slightly ahead of my right, and I rocked my body weight front to back causing a slight but noticeable wave in the ground.

My testing of the earth was akin to the countless teenage victims of horror movies. Those silly girls who are scared yet still tiptoe into the basement with no escape or slowly pull the blanket off what will be the corpse of their boyfriend. Always ill-advised, never smart. I should have quickly skedaddled from the yard and safely scaled the wood chip pile. Instead, I kept shifting my weight. And that's when the killer got me.

After the fourth or fifth time I shifted, my back foot dropped into the ground. Luckily I fell forward instead of backward as the ground, like a fault line in an earthquake, crumbled behind me. A small hole started by my foot escalated into an enormous sinkhole as the yard was being swallowed by the cesspool. The hole was growing in a line that was heading straight for the big tree that had kept the lawn from receiving sun.

The Cost of Living

I easily determined that had I not moved either the hole or the tree was going to get me. I made a run for the wood chips and, rather spastically, struggled to climb to the top. Jean pulled me up to the summit and the two of us watched as the tree collapsed into the cesspool and fell to its side, the top branches still visible above ground.

As it turned out, the sump in the backyard that had never collected water was now partially filled with sewage. The cesspool had burrowed a path beneath the house and came out the back side, as if Jean's home was going number two. I'd like to think it was sending a message for Jean to get rid of the shit in her house, but she took it as another sign. She now knew what to do with the wood chips.

We spent the rest of the day filling up the sinkhole with wood chips. With that one tree in the middle of her yard mostly gone, the ground received sunlight and grass began to grow - and grow and grow, never to be cut by Jean.

As I drove home that night, my clothes and skin stunk of wet stump. My spine needed to be adjusted and dabbing my armpits with car freshener just didn't cut it. I muttered the whole way, "Never again. Never again," but I knew those were hollow words.

— Chapter Fourteen —
THE COST OF
RUNNING A SMALL BUSINESS

When two people meet and fall in love, the equation is simple. One plus one equals happiness. Yes, I fell in love all over again. In what I chalked up to be a cosmic calculation of cataclysmic proportion, Jean also fell in love. While one and one can indeed add up to happiness, two and two totals catastrophe.

"Saturday night, eight o'clock," Greg told me. Okay, fine, I had caved in. Even though I had entered into a half dozen or more short relationships since that fateful night in Florida when I had dumped him, I still found myself comparing every man to Greg Mace. The results were never favorable for the other guy.

I began a career at an ad-buying agency, purchasing advertising time from local television stations in markets across the country, and advanced from assistant to associate buyer in only six months. The office was filled mostly with women who seemed to be split into two cliques – those who will get married and those who may not. The ladies in the "will get married" group were buying more than advertising time; they were biding their time until the right man came along, or even the wrong man, just so long as it was a man.

I belonged to the "may not get married" group. It's not that I couldn't picture myself in a white gown; it was just that I didn't feel this undying need to join myself with a faceless person in holy wedlock. Marriage never seemed real or within grasp for me, so I wasn't about to plan the rest of my life around it. This didn't mean that I wasn't going out with men or bedding them, but lately I had been waking up guilt-free and with a smile on my face. This was a new me; a carefree me, an adventurous me. And just when you think you have it all figured out, that you don't need some other person in your life to muck up the works, a colleague invites you for a weekend getaway to the Bahamas, where singles gather in some perverse courting ritual.

Feeling no obligation to comply with the unspoken rules of tropical matchmaking, I spent the whole weekend making a path between the surf and the tiki bar. I had already worked out in my head the painful rejection I would inevitably pass along to some unsuspecting man who chose to hit on the wrong woman.

"Listen, buddy, I came here for fun, and now you're stepping on that fun, so go step somewhere else." I relished the opportunity to use this bitchy attitude, which was unlike me, yet seemed wickedly fun and daring – especially knowing I would never have to lay eyes on any of these people again.

"Hey, you!" he said. I turned around ready to finally break a heart, but before one nasty word could pass my lips, my eyes took him in and my heart spoke volumes. It was Greg Mace.

The moment should have been uncomfortable, but it was quite the opposite. As it turned out, he had taken a job as an apprentice editor for movie trailers and a colleague had dragged him to the island. We were in the same boat.

"I've been asking myself why I ever agreed to come, and now it makes complete sense," he offered.

He didn't have to say another word. Serendipity had taken over. I clamped onto his neck and pressed my mouth to his. Without a conversation taking place, without any apologies or catching up, without any questions asked, Greg and I were back together.

And so, the weekend where I was supposed to play the part of cloudy skies looming over the heads of party-goers, preparing to downpour and wash away their fun, had turned into true blue paradise with the feel of a perfect honeymoon. Greg and I had both matured since our last encounter. Rebellious lust had given way to interludes of tender touches and snuggles. With our teenage years behind us, we had the unspoken trust of two adults who better understood the consequences of our actions. I returned to the contiguous states in a state of bliss. What I didn't expect was returning to find Jean in her own sense of euphoria.

Jean is in love. In love is Jean. Love is in Jean.

No matter how I mixed up those words, it didn't seem reasonable. Inexplicable to me, Jean had taken many suitors over the years, but never had she introduced me to a man whom I thought would be around for more than a couple of months... and they never were.

This time was different. This man was different. He was a cherubic man with sagging skin and a sagging self esteem. He was frugal, his conversations inevitably leading to a discussion of what things cost. He had lousy hygiene, never feeling the need to do more than run his fingers through his comb-over. He was Jean with a penis and larger breasts.

When the Internet craze started, I thought Jean would never show any interest. She didn't own a computer, nor did she show any desire to learn how to use one. Her lack of interest in anything technical coupled with the monthly charge for an internet service, seemed reason enough that she would not move with the times. However, I'd neglected to take into account that one of her friends would find a man in a chat room online and, most importantly, that the public library would eventually offer free online service.

I attempted to phone her one night and caught her just before she left the house.

"Where are you going?" I inquired.

"To the library." I immediately thought this to be strange, since Jean didn't read. As an accountant, she was good with numbers, but words escaped her.

"Why?" I was extremely curious. Perhaps there was a community meeting and Jean was getting involved in some serious issues. Maybe she was running a cancer awareness group. Most likely it was the free newspapers and coffee that had reeled her in; but the true reason she was heading to the library had never crossed my mind.

"To go online."

"Downloading coupons?" I kidded her.

"Ha-ha." There was a moment of silence, then, "Can you do that?"

"They have computers to let you surf online at the library?" This was news to me.

"What's surf?"

"To explore, click around, like channel surfing," I explained.

"Channel surfing?" She was about two generations behind the times.

"What do you do online?" I asked, sealing my eyes shut with disdain for myself as I realized it was a question for which I was unprepared to hear the answer.

"Promise not to get mad?" She didn't have to go any further. I knew what she was doing.

"Mom, you're not going into chat rooms, are you?"

She was, and she had been doing it for quite a while. She had not only emailed some of the men she met through these rooms, but she had already dated a few of them.

"Are you insane?"

"Why do you keep asking me that?"

"How can you possibly meet strange men online and go out with them? That's the dumbest thing you could ever do!" I was screaming out of frustration and fear, concern for her well-being. Jean was, if nothing else, very trusting. She believed most of what she was told and could be easily swayed to see a side of any argument, as long as that argument didn't come from me.

She calmly responded, "I don't know what the difference is if I go to some bar or go online. Everybody's a stranger until you meet them. Some strangers are just stranger than other strangers."

Sure, there was an acceptable yet twisted logic to what she'd said and I was about to bow to her reasoning, but then it occurred to me. "You meet men in bars?"

The Cost of Living

"No! But hypothetically." Somehow I felt she was retracting that last statement to avoid prolonging the conversation. This was a rude awakening. My mother went to bars. For all I knew, she was a barfly. It was safe to assume that she would only go on a designated Ladies Drink Free night, or would only consume liquor when someone else was paying for it. In either case, she was a patron of bars - to meet men. There was something so dirty about it. I couldn't help but picture her in a setting familiar to me, behaving just like I had when I wasn't with Greg, drinking gin and tonics, slurring her words in front of blurry guys who seemed cute for the moment, and then taking them home for a romp in the sheets, soiling the bed with the body fluids of a sweaty, hairy beast.

Damn! Suddenly, I felt dirty. I was admonishing myself for the sick behavior that I'd so brazenly called a social life. Jean made me feel guilty about myself without even trying. How did she do that?

"I'm perfectly safe about the whole thing, Caroline. I never give out my phone number and I only meet them in public places." She said this as if she spent days planning these clandestine trysts, drawing out maps with arrows, casing watering holes for the perfect escape route in case a rendezvous went awry.

"How do you know some sicko won't follow you home?" I half expected a rationale that was fully thought out. It would be just like her to plan for such contingencies.

"I hadn't thought of that..."

"Ah-hah!" I nodded knowingly, wagging my finger emphatically, even though she couldn't see me through the phone.

"Oh, poo. You're worrying about nothing. What would a sicko be doing on a computer?" She still believed the old notion that computers are only used by geeks in buttoned-down short-sleeved shirts hanging out of corduroy pants, wearing taped-up glasses. The real world knew that cyberspace hadn't merely given way to a revolution in commerce and information; it had also become a whole new playground for sexual predators.

"I think it's dangerous."

"Then how am I supposed to meet someone? A friend of mine is getting married next week," she offered.

"What does that have to do with it?" I asked.

"I can't go to a wedding alone." I could feel her near the door, wanting desperately to get to the library so she wouldn't miss out on the last good man available.

"Why not?"

"Because I was invited with a guest." Okay, there were two beliefs going on here. The first was that she needed to prove to the world that someone of the opposite sex wanted her. The second was that there were two meals to be eaten at the reception and "free is free, and you don't say no to free."

With her self-imposed deadline, Jean set off for the library that night and logged into a chat room called "Shopper's Delight." The only other chatter in the room went by the user name "Shu-In". The way Jean explained it, with no irony whatsoever in her tone, it was pre-destined chance encounter. In fact, they were two lonely people with a penchant for bargains who had sought each other out, sight unseen.

Stanley Shuper was his name, and being the protective, cynical daughter, I really wanted to know what his game was. He was somewhat of a bumbler, moving from one job to another. One might label him a Jack-of-all-trades, but that title would infer that he was good at everything, whereas Stanley seemed more like the type who was good at nothing. When Jean introduced us, Stanley was in his real-estate phase. Even though he had only recently passed the test to receive his license, Jean quoted him as if his word carried the same cache of a Bloomberg or Trump.

Jean's typical courtship consisted of Saturday night movies and the occasional dinner at a restaurant listed in her coupon book.

In Manhattan there is almost always an Asian immigrant stumbling through subway cars, trying to sell pathetic little toys to passengers. One always hides their eyes during these confrontations and I often wondered how anyone could make a living selling those plastic pieces of crap. In fact, I can't recall ever having seen a toy being sold. I have always felt that there are times and places for commerce; crowded trains are not one of those places. Hospitals, public restrooms and entertainment venues also seem inappropriate for solicitation, places one should be able to go without being approached by cheap product hawkers without permits.

It was during the time she was with Stanley that I discovered my mother was a pushcart peddler. Although I should have expected these moments to occur, this came as quite a shock because it involved a much more complex scheme than even Jean normally concocts. I had never imagined my mother as a nuisance to anyone other than me, but she had delved into a darker arena that made it even more embarrassing to be near her in public places.

Apart from the long ago summer she drove us back and forth between Flora & Bailer's, I had never witnessed another scheme to make money, only to save money. Those now cherished days had come to an end when I spotted her at a concert with a pillowcase full of merchandise.

During summers, Jean was a volunteer for "Friends of the Arts". The Arts were concerts performed on a great lawn in the middle of an arboretum from May through September. As a volunteer, Jean was assigned jobs such as ticket-taker, parking lot attendant, or usher for the outdoor performances. In lieu of pay, volunteers were allowed to watch the concerts for free, saving the $25 cost for a ticket. Although she had never heard of any of the bands that played at the arboretum, nor did she particularly enjoy the music, "free was free and you don't say no to free." In the end, she was getting something for nothing and that was all that mattered. If Pontius Pilate had offered free whippings, Jean wouldn't just be first in line, she would have figured out a way to obtain Jesus' thrashings as well.

The "volunteer concerts" were a major part of Jean's summers for over a decade. Once her boyfriend Stanley arrived on the scene, he was only too happy to join her; and in turn, Stanley introduced her to the "premium scam".

The premium scam is simple: "Premiums" are little gifts that salesmen give to customers as tokens of gratitude. These gifts, which can be office supplies or frisbees or traveling cups, t-shirts or yo-yos, etc., are usually imprinted with a company name so they can serve as merchandising giveaways. Many vendors promote their premium products this way at conventions.

Conventions are fairly easy to crash, and any average schmuck can walk around an exhibit hall or auditorium collecting free samples that bear the name "Jack O. Lanterns" or some such company. Stanley had apparently been infiltrating conventions for years, then selling samples at garage sales and flea markets for, one must assume, beer money.

When Stanley introduced Jean to the "premium scam," you'd think he had presented her with a 10-carat diamond engagement ring. If she had never achieved an orgasm before, she definitely achieved one then, which only cemented her belief that this man was her soul mate.

*   *   *   *   *   *   *   *

*   *

"I'll pick you up at 7:00, okay?" Greg had two tickets to see "The Allman Brothers". Death, addiction and age had not kept this band from playing for their faithful fans. It was always a good time and it had become sort of a recurring first date for us.

"Sounds great. Where?" I asked.

"The arboretum."

Dammit! From the first day my mother had begun to volunteer at the arboretum shows, every week she'd pestered me to go. "I can get you in free. Just wear black pants and a white shirt; I'll tell them you're helping me this week." Every week I would say no. For the most part, I was not a fan of the bands that played at the arboretum. They were usually some past one-hit wonder or a recent never-will-be, but every now and then a band I wanted to see would play there. Even so, I would still tell my mother "no."

My reasons for rejecting Jean's invitations date back to the time we'd snuck into the movie. While it's always nice to be handed a surprise gift, there's something distasteful about putting effort into getting something for nothing. It's like stealing. Moreover, I often found myself rejecting Jean because she pushed so hard for you to do things her way. I used to think it was because I wasn't taking advantage of "the deal," but soon realized that it had nothing to do with that. By rejecting her way of doing things, I was rejecting her. She was not receiving the validation she had sought all her life. Even knowing this, I still couldn't bring myself to accept her invitations to the arboretum shows. I was more than willing, however, to go as a paid attendee with Greg.

As we pulled into the parking lot I ducked down low, just in case my mother was working the cars that night. I don't know why I tried to hide. She knew Greg. She knew Greg and I were together again. It would only make sense that she would know I was in the car with him, hence hiding would be futile. Thankfully, she was not working the parking lot that night.

We walked through the entrance onto the great lawn, handing our tickets to the volunteer at the gate. This was not my mother either, which only meant that she was ushering. Since there were at least 30 ushers, chances were good that I could avoid running into her. When a prematurely balding young man escorted us to the front, I was able to relax and enjoy the show.

Halfway into the first set, as Greg Allman with his deep, raspy voice belted out "Melissa," I was enjoying the comforting love and sanctuary that I always felt in Greg's arms. It was a gorgeous, starry setting and I could only wish that my mother didn't volunteer there, so I could enjoy more such evenings at the Arboretum.

Then, suddenly, I heard her...

"See, she can do it. She only needed to be shown how."

That voice, the one that made my jaw clench, was no more than ten feet away. I should have closed my eyes and hid beneath Greg's jacket, but instead I looked over and saw Jean and Stanley carrying two pillowcases filled with who-knows-what, looming over a woman who was attending the concert with her Down's Syndrome teenage daughter. The mentally challenged girl was trying to work a yo-yo, a toy that had been forced into her hand by my mother.

"She loves it! And I have so many other things I could teach her to use," my mother claimed, rooting through her bag of goods.

One scam plus one scam equals infinite disaster. Having crashed conventions together since they'd become a twosome, Jean and Stanley had gathered a plethora of premiums and were now peddling them at the arboretum. Not only did my mother volunteer so she could get in free to concerts she had no desire to see, but she was actually shirking the volunteer work to sell crap to unsuspecting victims. Did she care that what she was doing was not only unethical, but also illegal? Apparently it had never crossed her mind that she needed a permit, and to make matters worse, she was forcing a toy into the hand of a disabled child to make a three-dollar sale!

The Cost of Living

"I'm sorry," the child's mother said, "I don't think she needs..."

"But look how happy the yo-yo makes her," Jean pushed.

I pointed the scene out to Greg, although I shouldn't have, because for him it was only another reminder that instead of marrying into this family and having Jean as his mother-in-law, he had the option of running in the opposite direction. I stood up and marched over to them, accosting my mother.

"What are you doing?" I insisted.

"What am I doing? What are YOU doing? Oh, C.C., you didn't pay to get in here, did you?" The air of disappointment in her voice almost made me choke on my words.

"You can't just sell those toys here, Mom. They're not even yours to sell."

"Of course they are!" she reasoned. "They were given to me. What difference does it make if I sell them here or at my garage sale?"

"You need a permit to sell stuff in public."

"Oh, poo!" She said this as if it countered all other arguments. As a mathematical theorem, "Oh poo!" was equal to the inverse relationship of common denominators. To put it another way, an axiom of our culture that didn't fit in with Jean's skewed sense of crazy could be countered by adding the unknown variable "Oh, poo!". Being a variable, there is no argument to disprove "Oh, poo."

She then leaned over to Stanley, as if they were spies working together in the field. "There's a family of five. Go sell them the rubber balls. Move it!" Stanley scampered off like a dutiful soldier.

"What is wrong with you two?" I asked. I think it was the first time I'd acknowledged that they were a couple.

"Me? You could have gotten in here for FREE. I am so disappointed." At this, she turned back to the Down's girl. "You like it, sweetie?"

The little girl rolled the yo-yo roll down her finger, but was unable to jerk it back up again.

My mother turned to me proudly. "See, I taught her that!"

The girl's mother rolled her eyes in a way that said, "Three dollars is a pittance if it gets this woman away from me." She retrieved her wallet and was ready to fork over the cash.

"Give her the yo-yo, mom," I pleaded.

"What? Are you nuts?" my mother practically screamed. "Why should I just give away a yo-yo?"

"You got it for free!"

Upon hearing this, the little girl's mother quickly placed her wallet back in her purse. "I don't think she needs a yo-yo tonight."

It was a stand-off. The girl's mother wanted the yo-yo for free and my mother wanted to make a profit – any profit.

"I'm not going to just give this to you," my mother stated emphatically.

"Ok, don't," the woman dared.

The Cost of Living

After a few moments of staring each other down, my mother growled and stomped away, leaving the toy behind for the girl. I assumed she had come to her senses and would feel good about bringing joy to a disabled girl's life.

"Mom," I caught up to her and grabbed her by the arm, turning her to face me, but before I could say anything she nastily snarled, "Who asked you to come here?"

Scared, I let go of her arm. She headed back to Stanley, who was collecting five dollars from his suckers of the moment. It was then that the Volunteer Director stepped up to my mother and Stanley and berated them for trying to sell their items at the show. He collected their pin-on volunteer badges and asked them to leave. I stood helpless as Jean collected her partner and stormed away in the opposite direction. After a minute or two I went back to Greg, but couldn't truly enjoy the rest of the concert. Jean's reaction had stunned me and I tried to understand why it had been so dramatic.

On the way back to the car I spotted Jean and Stanley packing up, like roadies after a gig. I had no idea how much they had pocketed that night, but I assumed it was more than their costs if you don't include gas or time. They hopped in the car and skedaddled out of the parking lot through a special "employee's exit."

Greg and I drove home quietly; the feeling that I had done something wrong was gnawing at me. My usual reaction would have been that Jean had once again intruded on my life and ruined my night, but instead I felt as if I had intruded and ruined her night. I did not need to be the "Jean Police." It was not my job to keep her from making adult choices, just as I had made it a point that she not trod on mine. The arboretum had become Jean's turf. She had laid claim to it long ago. Even so, her actions had infuriated me, and I couldn't let go. For the rest of the ride home, I ranted on and on about how she had ruined every possible good day of my life.

"I can't do this anymore," Greg said.

"So we won't come back here. The arboretum sucks anyway."

"No," he insisted. "This. This whole thing with your mother. You keep letting her get to you. You need help, C.C."

"What do you mean, help?" I asked. I couldn't imagine that he was talking about my mental health. I thought I had to be the most together person on earth after having survived all those years with Jean.

"You've got to let go. Maybe it's time to tell your mother, for your own sanity, that you just can't spend time with her anymore."

I suddenly reverted to the seven-year-old girl writing in the journal. "But she's my mother. We only have each other," I explained.

Greg nodded. "And that's why I can't be with you right now. When you figure it out, call me."

And that's how we left it. I didn't really believe that we were going to stop seeing each other again. I thought by now that he was finally in my life forever. I was mad at him at first, seeing him as a quitter. "If I can take it, why can't he?" That was reason enough not to call him the next day, and the day after that. I wasn't sure why I didn't pursue him by the third day, or by the end of the week or the week after that. In some way I understood him, but I didn't know why.

Three weeks later, I received a summons to appear in court. Apparently, I was being sued for selling licensed wares with trademarked company logos, without permission. Jean had been volunteering and hawking frisbees at another arts festival, only this time she was using an alias name and address – for one Caroline Kurchowski.

— Chapter Fifteen —
THE COST OF KEEPING PETS

Patches, 1978-1986.

Petey, 1986-1992.

Rocky, 1992-1993.

Leonardo, 1994-1995.

Candy, 1993-1998.

These were the pets that lived at one time or another with Jean and me. They all had different personalities and they all served a purpose. Most importantly, they were each in their time a part of my family. I mourn them still when I think of them and it was very hard to see them go. I thought Jean felt the same way, but recently I discovered this was not so.

"We're just not lucky with pets," she'd say.

Patches had been the first. She was a white mutt with a couple of black and brown patches, mostly on her face. She was a gentle dog who I am told slept under my crib to protect me. She was a constant companion who would follow me around, yet never got in the way. She was loyal and she loved me unconditionally, just as I loved her. She was like the normal mother I'd never had. There are times I wish I'd paid more attention to her, because when she passed away all I could think was that I hadn't had a chance to hug her one last time and let her know how much she'd meant to me.

Patches died while I was away at my sixth grade class trip to Washington, D.C. When I rushed out of the house, Patches sat at the front door as if to say goodbye. She was getting old. She had crust in her ears and her hair was dropping in clumps. It never occurred to me that she was really sick and wasn't going to greet me when I returned.

Instead, as I leaped into the house to relate wonderful stories about my excursion to the Capitol, I found myself pinned up against the corner by a half-golden retriever, half Labrador named Petey. I can honestly say I was terrified as this thin, yet imposing creature barked and snarled at me. Jean finally came down the stairs, pulled Petey away and introduced me to him. For a moment I was excited to think we now had two dogs, but the elation was gone with the knowledge that Patches was too.

The Cost of Living

"We're just not lucky with pets," she offered.

Petey was a pleasant dog. He liked to race around and retrieve balls and frisbees, and pretty much anything else you might throw past him. He was definitely more playful than Patches had been, but not nearly as compassionate or emotional, unless you were a couch, chair, or leg. Petey liked to hump, and if you were unlucky enough to fall asleep sitting up, you were sure to be awakened by a rather large canine thrusting his pelvis furiously against your limb.

One would think that this might have been his most disgusting habit, but it wasn't. Petey also had a gas problem. From the day Jean brought him home until the day he left us, Petey farted like an old man in the bathroom the morning after a dinner of beans and beer. The dog would lie down in one place, fart, and then move to another spot. After about ten minutes, he'd fart again and then relocate. When he wasn't eating or playing, Petey was farting and moving around the house.

It wouldn't have been so bad if his gas hadn't smelled so rotten. If we could have figured out a way to bottle up this smell and sell it to the Department of Defense, we would have been rich. Petey's gas could easily paralyze a crowd for up to two minutes. One friend of Jean's coined the nickname "Piggy Petey." It was a name that stuck.

Sadly, Petey came down with a debilitating disease that left his back legs completely immobile. He dragged himself up and down the stairs for months until he was simply too tired to do it anymore. The day Jean was to take him to the veterinarian, I was having my picture taken for the 9th Grade yearbook. My concern for Petey is forever etched on my face on page 216 just above the caption, "Nicest Smile". When I returned home, my mother informed me that the vet had said there was nothing that could be done and Petey had to be put to sleep. I cried on and off throughout that night. I never realized how much Petey had been a humorous fixture in our house.

"We're just not lucky with pets."

Jean wasted no time (well, thirteen hours to be exact) before she raced down to the animal shelter and replaced Petey with a shaggy little mutt named Rocky.

Rocky looked exactly like that sweet doggie film star "Benji," although looks can be deceiving, since Rocky was anything but sweet. Rocky was a menace to the entire neighborhood and could not be trained. He wasn't stupid per se. In fact, he was quite the opposite. Rocky was an exceptionally intelligent dog that basically had a "To hell with you!" attitude. He dug holes in the yard to escape. If I caught him just before he was about to dive beneath the fence, he would simply look at me, bark, and then be on his way. Every time he dug a hole, we would have to place a big rock or an old watering can or a piece of lumber to block it off. Replacing the fence with one that could do a better job of keeping him contained would have been too costly in Jean's eyes, so before we knew it the dog's yard was a complete eyesore, not unlike the rest of the property.

"Why should the dog live better than we do, anyway?" I surmised.

Exactly a year to the day that we'd adopted Rocky, he experienced a chronic coughing fit. I begged Jean to take him to the vet, but she insisted it was merely a hairball. Still, something did not seem right with him. I woke the next morning to discover Rocky laid out on the hallway floor. I didn't need to place a hand on him to know he was gone, but I did anyway. The little pain in the ass was stiff as a board. He must have been dead for most of the night.

I sat next to him for half an hour before noticing the small piles of vomit that adorned the house. I'd like to think it was my grief and not Jean's housekeeping that kept me from seeing them, but I can't be sure. Jean insisted that Rocky had been poisoned by some spiteful woman who hated the dog and complained incessantly about his trots around the neighborhood knocking over garbage cans. I had my own suspicions.

"We're just not lucky with pets." Or at least when it came to raising dogs, a rationale that came to her when she was passing by a little girl giving kittens away outside the supermarket. Jean preferred to think of it as an "impulse buy," even though she didn't pay anything. The kitten was beautiful, sleek with a thick coat of gray hair and the slightest dabs of white on the paws and mouth. Jean insisted we keep the kitten outside. It wasn't until the next week when I realized that to keep a cat inside meant buying a litter box and perpetually replacing the litter. Cha-ching!

"What's wrong with your cat?"

It had only been about a month and the kitten, who we were calling Grayson until we could think of something better, seemed to be adjusting to the outdoors. It was October and the nights were getting colder, but I had built Grayson a house made out of cardboard and stapled some old curtains to the outside to warm it up. When Grayson heard the glass doors to our back patio slide open, he peeked his head out of his little dwelling to see who it was. When those big green eyes met mine, he jumped out of his house and into my arms. It was a neat trick that I was bringing Beth home to see. Only this time, Grayson wasn't performing.

This time when I slid open the glass door, Grayson came tumbling out of his house like a drunk. This was when Beth asked her question, only I didn't have an answer as to what was wrong with him. All I could do was watch as Grayson tried to lift his head up and walk to me, only to have it fall to the ground while his body tumbled over it. I could see some mucous dribbling from his nose as I held him up and his eyes and head swayed side to side as if he were trying to focus but couldn't.

The Cost of Living

I pushed Grayson into Jean's hands the moment she got home from work. "I oughta sue that little girl for giving out sick cats," was how she responded.

"For what?"

"For mental duress," she said with a tone that insinuated I shouldn't have had to ask.

"Whose mental duress?"

"Yours obviously. You're completely unglued right now." I snatched the cat back.

"I'm concerned for the cat. If I sound unglued it's because of you. Don't you think we should call a vet?"

Jean grabbed the cat back, held him up, and studied his little face. Grayson's eyes were rolling every which way.

"Oh, please. I don't need a vet to tell me this little guy is simply fighting a cold. A little sugar water, a lot of love and I bet he'll be fine."

I convinced her to let Grayson stay in the house until he got better. After placing a shoddy litter box in the bathroom, I put Grayson to sleep under a cozy little doll's blanket nearby. For several days, when I opened the bathroom door to check on Grayson, he would come wobbling out, tripping over his own head.

Though the runny nose went away and Grayson was able to walk like a semi-normal cat again, he began to exhibit eccentric behavior. For one thing, he could never sit on a bare floor; something had to be on the floor that he could sit on. It could be a piece of paper, the phone cord, a tiny piece of string that was pulled from a sweater. It didn't matter what it was, Grayson needed to sit on it.

Then there was the David Letterman idiosyncrasy. Grayson loved to watch David Letterman on the television. From the moment he saw Dave's face on the screen until the show was over, Grayson was mesmerized and wouldn't budge from whatever he was sitting on at the time.

What made the Letterman thing even more peculiar is that we discovered that Grayson, from whatever illness he'd survived, had become deaf. Loud noises, screams, clanking of pots – he heard nothing. So we assumed it was Letterman's face that Grayson was attracted to.

When he finally seemed to be fully recovered, for the most part anyway, Jean decided it was time for Grayson to become an outside cat again. I worried for his ability to survive the cruel elements of the wilderness, but was told that Huntington, Long Island could not be considered the wilderness. After one night outside, I came home from school the next day to find Grayson gone. I was positive that he'd had met an untimely, gruesome fate at the hands of some neighbor's pooch. However, about an hour later a woman rang our doorbell. She was holding Grayson.

It seemed that Grayson had wandered into the middle of the road. Needing to sit on something on top of the road, he sat on the yellow dividing line. And he sat. And he sat. Even when this woman drove up behind him and beeped her horn for a good fifteen minutes, the cat didn't budge. How could she know he was deaf? Thankfully, she'd taken care of Grayson for the rest of that day before returning him to me. Jean now had no choice but to make Grayson an indoor cat.

"You sure he's not retarded?" Beth asked as she took a hit off the joint.

"He's deaf is all."

"It's the way his head bobs around. It makes him look like a tard." She started laughing. "That's what his name should be. Tard!"

"That is just so wrong!" I scolded, even though deep down I thought it was funny.

"How about Leonardo Retardo?" she suggested.

"I like Grayson."

"Oh, come on, it'll be like our joke. We'll just call him Leonardo, but we'll know Retardo."

I liked the idea of having that little secret, and when I tested it out on Jean, oddly enough, she liked Leonardo instead of Grayson. She thought Leonardo da Vinci had class, so it made the cat seem classy. I thought to myself, "Uh-huh, whatever."

So Leonardo spent two glorious years in the house with us. He was a good, quiet cat for the most part; one who watched Letterman and sat on pens. At dinner, Leonardo had this habit of climbing up my or Jean's leg. Since Jean was too cheap to de-claw the cat, the nails dug through our clothes and into the skin, and it hurt. Imagine having a polite conversation when something like that transpires — "So I went to my boss and I told him exactly what I wanted to say for years...AAAAAAAAAAHHHH!" And then a cat's head would pop up from your lap and swivel around at the food on the table.

It was during the summer when Leonardo suddenly seemed weak. At first he couldn't pick up his head and I thought that whatever had physically and mentally changed him from a Grayson to a Leonardo was returning to claim the whole cat. One day later, Leonardo could not pick himself up off the floor.

"Please, mom," I wailed, tears welling. "He needs a vet!"

"Just give him some sugar water. He's probably just dehydrated. If he's not better by next week we'll take him to the vet. I promise."

Sugar water? What was with the sugar water? Who would be stupid enough to think sugar water was a cure for anything? I was stupid enough. One would think that after years upon years of listening to Jean's advice, I would have seen through the charade. Water from the faucet and stolen packs of sugar from diners - that doesn't cost a thing, except a cat's life.

Dumb me nursed Leonardo with sugar water for another day. The next morning, Leonardo was missing from his cat bed (*cat bed n: empty box once used to store bulk supply of bagel-dogs with a remnant of a neighbor's shag carpet for a mattress. i.e. Don't throw out that box! I'll find a remnant and it will make a good cat bed.) I searched the rooms, diving under furniture, only to discover junk stored in every space imaginable. Then, upon opening the hallway closet, I discovered the ugly truth.

Deep within the corner recess of the closet, past the bales of magazines dating back a couple of decades, behind the tower of ragged towels and linens, laid Leonardo. To my surprise, which explained his condition, Leonardo was not alone. Three stillborn fetuses were with him. A fourth was still being pushed out.

Leonardo was miscarrying. Leonardo was not a he at all; he was a she. With all his... I mean, her... problems all her life, for some unexplainable reason we had always assumed that Leonardo aka Grayson was a boy. She seemed like a boy! But she wasn't. And on one of the rare occurrences when she'd slipped out the door, she had gone and gotten herself knocked up.

Leonardo never made it to the next week. She never even made it through the day. She died during the miscarriage and it was heartbreaking - to me. More than the passings of Patches, Petey, and Rocky combined, this one devastated me, probably because I'd felt that this unfortunate animal could not go it alone in the big cruel world. This pet was the one who could not survive on instinct. This was a creature who had needed me and I let him... I mean, her... down. Leaonardo's loss would never fade from my soul.

That memory came flooding back as I spoke to Jean about Candy. When I finally left her house, Jean adopted a chocolate brown labrador mix and named her Candy. Candy was a bright dog that seemed psychotically anxious to please. She needed a lot of petting, hugs and kisses. She would lay her head in your lap until she received affection. If that didn't work, she had this odd talent of actually pulling her mouth back into a smile and incessantly nodding until you paid attention to her. Thinking back on it now, Candy was not unlike most women with an inattentive boyfriend.

Regardless of her neediness, Candy was a good companion to Jean and it made me feel safe that my mother had the protection of an animal that truly loved her. So naturally it broke my heart when I paid a visit to them and saw that Candy's fur was dropping from her body in clumps, and her toenails had grown to the point where it looked like she was tip-toeing on shards of glass.

"When was the last time you took Candy to the vet?" I asked, already knowing the answer.

"I've been meaning to do that, but I just don't know where the day goes," Jean said.

I sighed in exasperation and loaded Candy and my mother into my car. We drove into town to the local veterinarian. One would think that the Kurchowski history of pet-rearing would put us on a first-name basis with the local animal doctor, but when your mother's primary medical solution is sugar water, you can bet that he had no paper record of any of our pets, and no mental record of my mother.

Dr. Corelli was a slender man in his sixties and the only veterinarian in our town. If one were casting a movie set in small town America in the 1950s, Dr. Corelli, with his meticulously combed hair, round specs and bow-tie, would fit the bill. He had black bushy arms and tops of hands, lending one to believe that caring for animals was a divine calling.

As he studied Candy and Jean, the Doc rubbed his chin in that way people do when they believe it's impossible not to remember something.

"She hasn't been here in a while, has she?" the vet inquired.

"Not... too... long," Jean answered, spacing the words just enough to make it seem like the exact date might actually come to mind if she could just recall what else she was doing that day. In fact, this was an out and out lie, since Candy had never been to the vet's office. Candy had received her shots at the shelter. She had also received a bath at the shelter. It is quite possible that the shelter had been the only health and hygiene care this poor dog had ever received.

Dr. Corelli grabbed Candy's hind quarters and felt around the muscles. He worked his way to her front, readying his fingers to raise her mouth so he could get a good look at the teeth.

"Has she been known to bite?" he asked.

Jean looked at me with a grin that said, "Get ready to be impressed."

"Candy, smile," she instructed. Candy did her odd trick and bared her teeth.

"Very nifty," Dr. Corelli said, although he didn't seem nearly as dazzled as even I thought he would be. His indifference was probably due to his newly established disposition that this was a woman who wasn't vigilant in animal care. While this was understandable to me, it left Jean with such distaste that she licked her lips as if preparing her discourse, a discourse of which I would be the lone audience member.

Sadly, Candy would soon learn that a smile does not necessarily save one from pain. The clipping of the toenails was especially harsh, which made me think about that famous picture in The Guiness Book of World Records of the Indian Gentleman with nails that had grown to the length of pythons. Imagine the disgusted look his mother received from the doctor when that guy had to finally get those things snipped.

Candy also received an injection. The dog looked my way with watery eyes that said, "Look what happens when you visit." It's true; pets do begin to look like their owners.

As for the hair that was falling out like she once worked as the security dog at Chernobyl, Dr. Corelli informed Jean that this was most likely due to either the kind of food the dog was fed or the shampoo used for the dog's baths. I quickly made a "Rain Man" assessment, rattling through the odds in my head, and determined it was definitely the food. If Jean bathed Candy at all, she wasn't about to buy shampoo. Most likely she thought water was fine. Of course the more likely scenario was that Jean didn't wash Candy at all. "Dogs ran around in the wild for thousands of years without bathing. I'm sure this is just a public relations scam designed by the water companies."

So, that left food. If Jean hadn't been feeding Candy, Candy would be dead from malnourishment. Here I was giving Jean the benefit of the doubt, for if it seemed reasonable to assume that dogs didn't need baths because they'd survived in the wild without them, then dogs could easily hunt for their own food. Since there hadn't been any reports of a mysterious, serial cat-killer on the loose, I had to assume that Jean was feeding Candy.

"What kind of food do you feed her?" the vet asked. He now wasn't even looking Jean in the eye when he addressed her. I was assuming he already knew the answer.

"Dog food. Regular food."

"Her skin is extremely dry and the hair follicles are brittle. You should feed her moist food, at the least those crumbly burgers," he instructed. "After a couple of months, hopefully this problem with the fur will go away. In the meantime, I'm going to prescribe a lotion for you to rub into her skin when you bathe her. This will help her heal faster." He handed my mother a prescription and we were on our way.

The moment I started the car's engine, Candy fell asleep in the back seat, not unlike an exhausted toddler who screamed his head off after receiving an inoculation. It took only a right turn out of the parking lot before Jean felt she was well out of earshot to begin her rant.

"What a quack!" she exclaimed. I actually spit trying to hold in a laugh.

"What's so funny?"

"Nothing," I said. "Just you, calling a vet a quack."

"I don't get it."

"He's a vet. An animal doctor. You called him a quack."

"I still don't get it."

"A duck quacks..." I prodded. She pursed her lips and shook her head. I tried to explain. "A duck quacks. A duck is an animal. He's an animal doctor."

"That's a stretch," she critiqued.

"Yeah, well, it loses something on the third explanation."

"Anyway, I'm never taking Candy back to that..." She chose her words more carefully, "...that nut again."

"Why? What did he say that was so bad?"

"He basically accused me of killing the dog."

Killing the dog? And she accuses me of stretching my words?

"He just thinks you need to take better care of her; and you do. You always bought that cheap, generic food for the dogs. I cringed every time I heard their teeth crunch down on it." I began to think about all the dogs we'd had and that sound they made trying to get their food down to a size where they could swallow it. Suddenly those sounds seemed much more pronounced in my head. Crunch, crunch, crunch. Stones of food dropping from their mouths to the floor, eventually licked up by their thick, slobbery tongues only to go crunch, crunch, crunch once again until they turned into edible pebbles.

"That dog food is fine. They wouldn't sell the food if it was bad for them," she determined. "And I've never heard of getting a prescription filled for a dog. It's not like I can put Candy on my health insurance. I'm sure I can pick up some lotion over the counter that will help her skin."

"Why don't you just get the dog the medicine she needs?"

"What she needs is a good brushing to get all the bad hair out that's infecting the good hair, a nice shampoo, and a bowl of sugar water," she explained in a slow affectation.

And this is when I made the connection. The last time I had heard the term "sugar water" was when Jean had prescribed treatment for Leonardo. Perhaps it had been years of denial, but I couldn't block it out of my head any longer. It was so obvious in that moment, even though I had been so oblivious before.

"Sugar water cannot cure an illness! You're killing the animals!" I accused her.

"Ssssh! C.C.! How could you?" It was a knee-jerk reaction to my accusation. First she tried to quiet me, like a desperate criminal hiding from the law. Then she returned her own accusation, as if I was wrong for having thought such a thing.

It was too difficult to swallow any longer, and that's when the bigger truth hit me. This one wasn't a little smack to the cheek. This was a sledgehammer to the skull.

"You didn't want to pay the veterinarian."

She jerked her head back and wrinkled her brow. "What?"

"That's why, isn't it? You're too cheap to pay for the animal doctor."

"Caroline, I am not cheap," she insisted without the tiniest bit of irony.

"Fine. You're frugal. Thrifty. Niggardly."

She slapped my face. "Don't use that term around me. I won't accept it from the neighbors and I certainly won't accept it from you."

I didn't cry from the slap. I didn't get angry. I said, calmly and cautiously, "It means cheap."

"I am not cheap."

"Oh no? How long did Petey drag his dead legs up the stairs before he died? Two weeks?"

"I thought he would get better," she said.

"And Rocky? He was coughing like an old man for how long?"

"That was a hairball!"

"CATS get hairballs!"

She wrinkled her brow at me again. "They do?"

"And speaking of cats, what about Leonardo?" I asked.

"Leonardo? He was mentally and physically challenged from birth. How is that my fault?"

"It's your fault," I explained, "because you didn't want to pay to treat him... her... whoever."

"C.C., do you know how vets make their money? By getting you to buy their shampoos and collars and medicines. Candy sheds. All dogs shed. So Candy does it a little more than others. I'm supposed to believe some guy who couldn't make it through a real medical school? How do I know if he's telling the truth?"

"You're not a vet," I said.

"So how do I know he knows what to do?"

I starting shaking uncontrollably. "BECAUSE HE IS A VET!"

She rolled her eyes back into her head as if she couldn't believe I wasn't comprehending her rationale.

I covered my eyes. "Oh my God, oh my God! I can't believe this! You killed my pets! And for what? To save a few bucks?"

She waved me off. "We're just not lucky with pets."

As we pulled into her driveway and got out of the car, I tried to remain calm. "No, mom. People aren't lucky with the horses. People aren't lucky at bingo. People aren't lucky in love... But this is not about luck. It's about not properly caring for them because YOU'RE CHEAP."

As she entered the house, Jean turned to face me defiantly, her arms crossed. "Money has nothing to do with it."

"Oh no? Then buy the gourmet dog food."

"That's ridiculous."

"Mom, I swear. Either buy the gourmet dog food or I will not step foot in this house again."

"Oh, please! You won't come here because of dog food?"

And then I exploded. It all came out, a typhoon of disgust.

"It's not just the dog food, Mom. It's the boxes of shit everywhere. It's the expired food in the cabinets, the moldy bread on the counter, the fungus growing in the showers, the crumbs in the carpet, the freebies you accumulate, the washing machine that doesn't work, the smell of your clothes that haven't been washed, the three busted televisions lined up along the walls of the den, the stacks of magazines that could be made into a whole other house, the used furniture that nobody uses. You need help. You need to realize that the way you live, it's not living. It's just – barricading yourself with junk. This... this isn't healthy." I took a deep breath.

"You're such a good person, mom. Not a lot of people have told you that. But I love you. And if you loved yourself just a little, maybe all this would go away."

The Cost of Living

I wanted to hug her, but this was one of those tough love moments and I had to be hardcore. She looked at me, penetrating my eyes to see just how serious I was. The pendulum was swinging and I wasn't sure which side it was going to stop on.

"Fine. I get it," she said, raising her hands in defeat.

"Really?"

"Yes. I'll add water to the dog food to make it moist."

I shook my head. It was no use pursuing the conversation any longer.

"Goodbye, Mom," I practically whispered as I headed for the door. There was something definite in my voice. I honestly wasn't sure when I would see her again. I wasn't sure I ever could.

"I'll call you later," she yelled after me.

But she didn't. We were in a stalemate position, and neither of us wanted to make the next move.

—— Chapter Sixteen ——
THE COST OF CARE

Eight months. It was eight months since we had spoken. Jean had left a few messages on my answering machine, but only when she was certain I wouldn't be home. I, in turn, would call her emergency cell phone, knowing that she never turned it on. We were quite a pair.

It was childish, yes, but I wasn't sure if I could ever have a relationship with a woman whose priorities seemed so completely out of whack. I swore to myself that it would take a catastrophe to bring us together again. That catastrophe turned out to be the return of Jean's cancer.

I pressed the answering machine's PLAY button. "Hi, C.C., it's mom. Bad news. Cancer's back. Call me. Bye." That's how she put it, like she was telling me my grandmother was in town.

Of course, my mother had made me so cynical of her true intentions that I wasn't entirely convinced she hadn't claimed cancer just to open up the channels of communication and force me to call. Or, maybe she'd performed some kind of voodoo, to conjure up the cancer's return. That would be just like her... Then, a moment after it popped into my brain, I hated myself for even thinking it; and if I didn't hate myself enough then, I certainly peaked in self-loathing when I learned she wasn't pretending.

I escorted Jean to the surgeon's office, to go through many details of the impending procedure that she'd been through before. She actually appeared quite chipper on the ride over. I wasn't sure if this was in response to anxiety, an attempt to keep me from worrying, or because in some sick way Jean enjoyed having cancer. I know how disturbingly twisted that sounds, but this was a woman who craved attention and love. Psychologically beaten down by her own mother and my father, and perhaps countless others I knew nothing about, Jean's core spirit had been crafted and driven by an insatiable need to be noticed. Her hoarding, her house, her wood chips - they all screamed "Look at me!"

The Cost of Living

As I'd witnessed from her last bout of the big C, Jean was willing to talk about her cancer with anyone who would listen, offering up a flash or feel of the fake boob that occupied the space of the one that had been cut loose.

When we arrived for her appointment, Jean went through the blood pressure and weigh-in routine before sitting down with the surgeon. He had little to say, other than to be fairly matter-of-fact about the situation. There was little surprise in his mind that the cancer had returned, so lopping off knob number two seemed to have been on his calendar for quite a while.

Strangely, this surgeon seemed to be a bit dismissive. It was as if he was trying to push us out of his office. Frankly, I was becoming a bit irritated by his demeanor, especially when he stood up as if to say, "That's all you'll get from me. See you when I take your breast."

Taking his cue, I also stood. Jean didn't. She pulled a thick folder from her suitcase-purse and proceeded to interrogate him.

"I was researching online and wondering if it is truly necessary to have this procedure. There was one website that listed ten answers to find before losing your breast. I think we should go over this checklist, don't you?"

With a deep sigh, the surgeon fell back into his chair, rubbing his eyes. I could sense now why he'd been trying to hurry us out. I sat back down.

"Number one...," she began.

He interjected more or less right away, "Mrs. Kurchowski, I am your surgeon, not the Cosmo.com health editor. We've put you through numerous tests and scans. I have been seeing you for years; this is not a snap judgment. You need to either trust me, or go to someone else."

Jean looked up and stared straight at him. He put up his hands and raised his eyebrows, as if to say, "It's your choice." She placed the folder back into her bag.

"I see," she said, and she stood up to leave.

"Please schedule your pre-operative testing with the nurse at the desk before you leave. I'll see you at the hospital next week."

I followed Jean out to the front desk, where they cordially scheduled her pre-op blood work for the morning before the operation.

She asked the nurse, "Can you do me a favor? When they do the blood test, can you ask them to check my metabolism? I think something's off."

The nurse looked up. She looked to me, then back at Jean. "Excuse me?"

"My metabolism. Can they check that? Because I've been dropping eleven pounds and putting on eleven pounds regularly for years now. I think something's off."

It was an awkward moment as Jean waited for a response to a question the nurse had never heard before. Finally, I broke the silence.

The Cost of Living

"It's not your metabolism. It's the bagel-dogs. And the Ring Dings. And the ice cream." The nurse couldn't help but laugh. Jean looked at me with fire in her eyes. I tried to make the moment less tense. "Don't worry, next week you'll lose a few pounds when the breast comes off." Jean swiped her paperwork up and stormed out.

The car ride home was uncomfortable. I hadn't meant to make light of the situation, but I could see Jean had made a name for herself in that medical building and I couldn't wait to get her out of there. I assumed that since the disease hadn't turned her mood dark, laughing at the cancer was open game. But, I was wrong. This was her cancer. She made the rules, and that was her right.

On the morning I was to drive Jean to the hospital for her second mastectomy, I woke up with a pain that was so excruciating I wanted to scream. Except I couldn't. My uvula was so swollen it had slid into my esophagus and I was gagging for air. At five in the morning, with intense discomfort, I was clutching my throat. I needed the Noah's Ark of painkillers, something that would knock me into a coma for the next forty days and forty nights. I knew I needed to see a doctor, because it's simply not normal to wake up at five in the morning suffocating on your own uvula. Between the sound of gagging and my hands wrapped around my throat, had someone walked in it would have seemed as though I was literally strangling myself.

I was running a fever of 104 degrees. My body was clearly fighting some kind of infection. However, I wasn't about to run to the emergency room, since I was heading to the hospital soon anyway.

Many times I'd found that my reactions to Jean were due in large part to my fear of how her odd behaviors reflected on me. Now, however, with my swollen uvula descending deeper into my body, I caught myself thinking about how I was in fact, genuinely worried about her, and that made me feel selflessly good about myself. Although her behavior was maddening on a daily basis, I truly loved my mother. "I am a good daughter," I commended myself; but then I quickly realized that I was back to superficially thinking about me and how this selflessness made me feel so humble, which, once you acknowledge it, is the exact opposite of humble.

This kind of rambling introspection enabled my mind to wander because, truth be told, I was frightened that Jean's operation would not go well this time. The cancer had returned and Jean was about to go through a second operation along with doses of radiation. This could very well be the beginning of the end for her, and my own health mattered none.

Or so I thought…

The throbbing and swelling in my throat grew to a point where I couldn't utter a single word without a scream that was only deadened by gagging on that damn uvula. I was feeling clammy from the fever and my eyes every now and then would roll back into my head. My body was trying to shut down in an attempt to fight the infection, but I used every bit of energy I had left to stay awake and conscious, hoping to ensure that Jean was comfortable before being wheeled into surgery.

"Would you look at this room? The wallpaper is peeling."

Just like my room at home, I thought, because Jean had insisted on wallpapering my bedroom herself. "Who needs a professional?" she'd explained to me when I was too young to spot the trend in her logic. "It's pasting. You paste in kindergarten. You're going to tell me a grown woman can't paste?"

It turned out that a grown woman could paste, except that this particular grown woman could only do it badly. The wallpaper was so lumpy that there were times when I would scale my walls pretending to be a rock climber. Within a week, every corner of the wallpaper had started to peel away from the wall. Jean's attempts at re-pasting proved futile, and eventually she pulled out the industrial strength stapler. My room had wallpaper with decorative steel seams running down the walls like mini railroad tracks.

"And the vinyl on that chair is ripped," she continued. "Where does all this insurance money go?"

"To making you healthy, Mom." I said this through clenched teeth due to the pain of my esophagus when I made any sudden movements.

Unfortunately, Jean took my altered speech as anger.

"Don't get pissy with me. This is not the time to get pissy."

"I'm not getting pissy," I whispered calmly, trying hard not to sound angry. At this point I was hoping she'd ask me what was wrong, so we could get it out of the way and yet I wouldn't be burdening her with my troubles, but she didn't ask.

I began to put her things away for her as she changed into a blue cotton hospital gown. Before I could turn my head, I could see the reminder of the previous operation. I'm not sure if it was the fever or the sight of this frailty in my mother, but I began reeling and had to grab the arm of the ripped vinyl chair to maintain my balance.

"Can you get a nurse for me?" For a moment I thought I had requested the nurse, but it was Jean.

"Why? What's wrong?" I asked.

"What's wrong? That chair. This room costs a lot of money. Didn't we just have this conversation?" she said as if I had lost my mind.

"You're not paying for the room. Insurance is."

"And I pay for insurance. You know what, don't get the nurse. Don't do me any favors," she said as she got into bed. She was suddenly playing the part of the martyr, the same part I had been playing since I'd woken up that morning. We were playing the same game, except my motives were altruistic while hers were filled with guilt. Either way, they yielded the same result. I went to get her a nurse or another chair.

The Cost of Living

I'm not entirely sure how far I actually got. I may have been on my way back from retrieving the chair. I may have reached a nurse and inquired about a chair. What I do remember is exiting Jean's room, turning a corner into the hallway, and squinting past the florescent lighting that glared off the slick surface of the floors. Those lights made me dizzy and I could feel my eyelids grow heavier as I worked to regain focus. There was nothing I could remember after that. My guess is that I fainted not far from my mother's room.

When I woke, I was extremely disoriented. It took me a moment to realize that I wasn't in my own bed. I nervously glanced around, very weary, hoping and praying that I wasn't waking up from a drunken night's misjudgment. Then I turned my head and saw a balding, middle-aged woman lying in a hospital bed next to me.

"Howdy-do!" she said with a smile and a wave. She seemed mysteriously happy for someone in a hospital bed. Out of politeness I tried to wave back, and noticed the intravenous line stuck in my arm. I tried to say hello to her, but couldn't speak.

"Don't even try, honey. You're just gonna hurt yourself. I'm Miriam. We're roomies - at least until one of us gets better or dies." She let out a cackle and a snort. "Just kidding. I wouldn't have said that if you weren't gonna be fine."

"Wha——" I tried to mutter, but quickly swallowed the pain.

"What happened?" she guessed.

I nodded.

"Ho, brother, sister. You passed out cold; hit your head on the floor. I heard you looked like your bones just left your body and your skin flopped to the ground. Everybody in the hospital's talking about it. You're the girl who was visiting her mother and passed out cold."

"Wha—" This time I could have finished the thought, but Miriam jumped to finish it for me.

"What's wrong with you? Well, that's between you and your doctor, but from what I heard, you had abscessed tonsils. Completely infected. You know, you really shouldn't come to the hospital if you're sick... Unless of course you're being admitted."

"How—"

"How's your mother? Don't know. A nurse said she was gonna find out for when you woke up. Guess they didn't expect you to wake up so soon, but I'm glad you did. I was getting a little bored.

"My kids live in Colorado, so I don't really have anyone to visit me. They wanted to fly in, but I told 'em that I only have a hernia. Why bother? Look, this isn't my first time in the hospital, and it won't be my last. When it is my last, they can fly in for the funeral services. Besides, I always end up with some roommate who I can abba-dabba-dabba with, you know what I mean?

"Yesterday there was a lovely woman in your bed who was here to get one of those balloons put in her heart. Anyway, so I'm sitting here chatting with her... just a lovely, lovely gal... and then I realize she's being rather quiet. Dontcha know, she's dead. Imagine there was a dead woman in that bed not twelve hours ago! But, now I have you, and listening to the docs talk about your condition, I'd say we're going to be bunking together for quite a while."

"Please..." I was finally able to choke out.

"Save your voice, honey. Do you like TV? Because I don't. Art of communication!" She pounded a fist into the pillow to emphasize each syllable. "That's the problem with you young people today. You lack verbal communication skills because of TV."

I thought to myself, "No, you stupid twit, I lack verbal communication because infectious bacteria has commandeered my throat." Thankfully my fever returned, and I drifted back into a coma-like state.

Clearing my blurry eyes a few hours later, I turned my head to the side and into focus came Miriam. She waved with a big, stupid grin on her face. I turned away from her and sitting on the other side of my bed was Jean. She was fully clothed with her pocketbook held neatly in her lap. I had to be dreaming, because there was no way she should have been up and around. She was scheduled to be in the hospital for at least ten days, even if all went well.

"How you feeling, sweetie?" She placed a hand on my shoulder.

In a scratchy voice due to the pain that still overtook my throat, I asked, "What's today?"

"Thursday."

"What's the date?"

"The 16th."

Why was she not providing me with all the information? Was she trying to torture me?

I pursed my lips. They were very dry and I swallowed hard. "Month. Year."

"June 16th, 2004." I squinted, trying to figure it out like an algebraic equation. Only one day had passed? How was this possible? I asked her, "They released you?"

"Oh, no, I didn't have the operation." She said this so nonchalantly, like she'd just turned down a facelift. Didn't have the operation? How was this possible?

"What went wrong?"

Jean laughed. "What went wrong? You almost died, silly. Your tonsils burst and the abscess, the infection, went into your throat. They said if you hadn't been in the hospital at the time, you'd probably be dead. So if I didn't have cancer, you'd be dead. Ha! Can you imagine?"

I could hear in her voice that this was a great story for her to tell her friends. I imagined her sitting at the library, knitting, "My C.C.! She's so lucky I had cancer. If it wasn't for my disease, she'd be dead. Good thing that cancer came back."

The Cost of Living

"Mom, you have to have your operation. What did the doctor say?"

"Oh, piddly-poo. Who is he to tell me the cancer could rapidly spread?"

"Mom!"

"C.C., I'm much older than you are. You're my baby. You'll always be my baby. I need to know that my baby is safe. That's my job. Your infection will be gone in a few days, and a few more days won't kill me." Then she shrugged, realizing. "Well, hopefully it won't."

Jean sat there, day in and day out, right by my side. We mostly watched T.V. together and I slept a lot. Even though I was surviving a near-death experience, it was the most comforting time of my life.

Four days later, with the infection under control, I was ready to be released. Due to hospital policy, I had to be taken by wheelchair to be discharged. Jean accompanied me as I signed the final paperwork and was wheeled outside. Once we were past the sliding glass doors, I got out of the wheelchair and Jean got into the wheelchair and the nurse took her back up to her room.

The next morning, Jean had her mastectomy. The doctor said the operation seemed to go well, but like all breast cancer patients, Jean would need mammographies and check-ups every year for five years, to be certain the cancer hadn't spread. It was only then that she'd be in the clear.

213

As we spent the next ten days in the hospital, this time I played the role of comforter; but it was difficult for me. She looked paler than after the first operation and I could tell this go around had taken more of a toll, both physically and mentally. Luckily, I was better prepared to cheer her up. This time I didn't clean anything in the house. She returned home to the same chaos she'd left it in.

I led Jean to the couch and laid her down. She reached for the remote and grimaced from the pain. I grabbed for a pillow, unsure what I was supposed to do with it.

"Are you okay?"

She bit her lip and nodded, "I'll be fine. I'm just so worried about pulling out these staples."

"Ewwww, yuck, don't go there!"

"It's no big deal. Do you want to see it?"

I leaned away from her. "See what? Your missing breast? No. Just turn on the T.V. and relax. I'll go out and grab us some lunch."

I left her with the remote control and a glass of water. I grabbed the keys and went outside. There was a Greek restaurant she loved where you could get lamb Gyros for five dollars. It was delicious and the only sandwich Jean thought worth splurging on.

As I was getting in my car, I saw a landscaper's truck and trailer pull up across the street. Three young hispanic men emerged, quickly unloading their equipment. I looked at my mother's craggy lawn, with the centerpiece tree surrounded by the woodchips that had somehow appeared like a designed sculpture, and had an idea. I approached the eldest looking landscaper and asked what he would charge to cut my mother's lawn. I explained how she'd just returned from the hospital, so maybe he could help us out. He said for ten dollars they would cut and edge the lawn. He promised not to touch the sculpture for fear of breaking it. I nodded in agreement and told him I would be back in fifteen minutes.

By the time I'd bought the Gyros and returned, the landscapers were just getting started. I entered the house to see Jean holding her side, staring at the men through the back door.

"What are they doing?"

"Mowing the lawn. I saw them across the street and they said they'd cut the lawn for ten dollars," I explained. I assumed Jean would be ecstatic at "the deal."

"I can mow the lawn. I don't need to waste ten dollars," she said.

I couldn't believe she would even think about putting up a fight. "But you don't. You can mow the lawn, but you don't."

I unwrapped her lunch and put it on the coffee table. "Eat," I demanded.

"Ten dollars... Ridiculous." I shook my head and left her to eat her lunch, finding some chore I could do while calming down. Instead of being grateful, all she could do was criticize, and it still struck a nerve.

When I heard the mowers turn off and being loaded back onto the trailer, I rushed outside to pay them. Since ten dollars couldn't be split evenly between the three men, I gave them fifteen. They thanked me, since it was fifteen dollars they wouldn't have to tell their boss about; they could keep it for themselves. In hindsight, I wish I had given them more.

I walked back up the driveway, admiring the freshly cut lawn, when I saw Jean standing by the front door examining the work they'd done.

"It looks good, right?"

"It does." I was shocked that she agreed - then came the kicker. "Why did you give them fifteen dollars?"

I was taken aback. I shook my head. "What?"

"I saw you give them three five-dollar bills. You said it was only ten. You lied to me."

"I didn't lie. It was supposed to be ten, but there were three of them. So they each got five dollars. What's the problem?"

She took a bite of her Gyro and mumbled in a way that was supposed to shame me, "Fifteen dollars…"

I did the math. For all the days I planned to be there during her recovery, it was going to cost me a little more than a dollar a day to hear her complain about this. It wasn't worth it, but at least it seemed as though Jean would be fine.

— Chapter Seventeen —
THE COST OF
SAYING GOODBYE

I couldn't start Jean's eggplant minivan that morning. The engine just wouldn't turn over. Finally, after a few "cachinks" it kicked in. After backing out of her driveway and driving about a quarter of a mile down the slick, ice-patched road, I realized the car wouldn't accelerate past 25 miles per hour. Luckily, a service station is situated at the end of Jean's street.

The mechanic on duty was Vinnie The Schneak. As he surveyed under the hood he reminisced, like always, about the first time we'd met and how if it wasn't for him giving me a hard time with my bike, Greg and I never would have gotten together. I just nodded and smiled as he seemed to validate his special gift for bringing lovers together.

I actually felt sad for Vinnie The Schneak. Even back on that fateful day, the way he acted on that bike trail, it was obvious he'd been seeking attention and, more likely, affection. Eventually his friends had matured in ways that Vinnie The Schneak never did. He'd never had anyone in his life. I assumed it made him feel good to know that he was a part of two people experiencing those feelings so that he might have them too. I felt a sudden, strange desire to help Vinnie.

"I bet if Greg didn't get you, I would've." Ok. Desire gone.

Upon finishing his inspection, Vinnie the Schneak, wiping his greasy hands with an oily rag, concluded that Jean hadn't had a tune-up since she'd purchased the car ten years ago. I could hear her voice in my head. "A tune-up? What's that? Do you know what epilepsy is? It's when you have a seizure and the doctors don't know why. So is that what a tune-up is? When the car needs to be fixed and you don't know why? I'm supposed to pay for an epileptic car? No thank you!" Hearing her thoughts actually brought a tiny, comforting smile to my lips.

I explained to Vinnie the Schneak that I was late, that I had to get to the hospital. He sensed the immediacy in my voice.

The Cost of Living

Vinnie the Schneak serviced the car with a few wires and a new set of spark plugs and had me on my way. He offered me a ten-percent discount, I suspect out of pity. It didn't matter. It was Jean's car. Out of some sort of homage to her, I had to accept it.

By the time I finally arrived at Jean's room on the oncology floor, I was able to compose myself and even force a smile on my face. Jean was asleep, so I sat next to her bed. The remote control for the television was still clutched in her hand. I grinned knowing that she was enjoying her favorite programs after I'd argued with her for a full hour that she should just pay the ten dollars to connect the TV. I glanced around the room at the many flowers and giraffe pictures that adorned the rolling shelf table, windowsill and nightstand. She'd certainly let her friends know after all these years what her likes were.

I studied Jean's face for a solid hour as she quietly slept. Her face and arms were ashen and she was gaunt. Ironically, she'd finally lost all the weight she'd been promising herself she'd lose. She seemed serene, even as the cancer was eating up her insides. Unable to dye her hair, her head was now mostly silver and I wondered aloud why she hadn't let it go natural long before. She was more beautiful with gray hair. I reached out and gently stroked it. Maybe seeing her locks this color allowed me to rationalize that she'd lived a long life.

I reflected back on a year ago when I'd wrongly predicted that Jean was going to be fine. Instead, the cancer had spread quickly. I certainly was thankful that I hadn't made that prediction out loud, since Jean was sure to say, "See. I'm dying. You were wrong again. Oh, C.C., what are you going to do without me?" In only 17 days, Jean had been reduced to an "any day now" patient; and "any day now" was going on day four.

She woke up after about an hour and without missing a beat, changed the television station. A "Seinfeld" rerun was airing and I allowed her to watch for a little bit before letting my presence be known. Every now and then she emitted a breathless giggle. When one of the characters did something she didn't approve of, she said, "Oh, that's not right." I couldn't help but laugh, and Jean's head turned on the pillow. She'd caught me.

"How long have you been sitting there?"

"Not long," I replied. "Did you eat today?"

"I'm so dizzy. And those damn nurses. Every time I nod off, they come in and wake me up to take my blood pressure. You'd think they could come back."

"They're probably on a schedule," I surmised.

"They're on a schedule? I think my schedule's a little tighter than theirs."

Although I knew she was wrong, in a way she was right. I also knew that, even as she lay dying, Jean was not going to make life any easier.

The Cost of Living

The next day seemed to come too quickly. As the only next of kin, it was my duty to take care of the arrangements. I considered asking my grandmother if she'd like to partake in planning the funeral, but that would only be inviting someone to tell me what an awful job I was doing. Part of me felt that perhaps that wasn't such a bad idea, since it would seem that Jean was still with me, but I rightly thought better of it.

The Shapiro Funeral Home wasn't far from Jean's house. Many questions were asked and many details were decided, but I felt like I was in a perpetual blank stare. The funeral director snapped tissues from the holder on his desk. "Should we take a break?"

I shook my head and waved him off with my hand. "No, let's get this over with."

"Caroline?" I knew that voice right away. It was Beth. She was standing in the doorway. I ran into her arms and screamed into her shoulder. The pain was suddenly terrible.

"Thank you," was all I could say.

The funeral director escorted us to the coffins. He waved his arm fluidly, like a car dealer in a showroom. "Take a look," he said. "If you have any questions…"

Beth and I stepped from one to the next, sizing up the options. There were elegant caskets with brass holders, silk curtains, pewter plaques. None of them felt right to me. I looked at Beth and shook my head.

"If you're having trouble deciding, I often ask which casket would the loved one feel most comfortable in?"

The answer was so easy, Beth and I said it at the same time. "The cheapest one."

The funeral was simple. Other than me, Beth and my grandmother, Jean only had her small group of friends, some of the same people who'd spent holidays with her and some others I had never met, but somehow imagined I knew. They were all genuinely sad and had seen Jean in ways that I had not been able to. My frustrations with a woman who'd obsessed over money and surrounded herself with junk was myopic at best. There had also been a fun and caring side of Jean, the side a person's good friends see and automatically associate with that individual. She hadn't been as alone as I'd thought.

I looked down at my mother's tombstone, at the words "Born 1951, Expired 2005." I cocked my head as I stared at the word "Expired". All I could think was what Jean might have said.

"Don't throw me out. I'm still good."
I hoped nobody caught my smirk.

That night, I drank a bottle of wine as I sat in a candle-lit room, staring at the walls of my apartment. They were purposely bare - uncluttered is how I liked to call it. I'd made it a point to not fill every inch of my rooms with "stuff". However, in being so careful to avoid clutter, I hadn't allowed myself to enjoy shopping and expressing my taste or sense of style. I had decorated in a completely opposite, minimalist direction, and I wasn't sure now how I felt about it. I just kept staring at the wall. It was crying out that it needed something. It was naked. I promised that wall that I would buy it something nice to wear.

As I was speaking to my apartment, there was a knock on the door. I got up and actually sauntered through the corridor, opened the door, and found Greg standing in the stairwell. He was shaking his head with his lips pursed in a way that said, "I'm sorry and I don't know what to say."

I smiled and fell softly against his chest, my exhausted arms dangled over his shoulders. "Thanks for coming. I hope I didn't pull you away from anything, I said.

"Well, I had a date with this woman from my office..."

I looked up at him with 'are-you-serious?' eyes.

"No, really," he added. "But it was just one of those got-nothing-better-to-do dates, and now I've got something to do." He was so matter of fact about it. He had been waiting for my call for a long time.

I laid my head back down on his chest and we walked clumsily into my apartment and to the couch that way. I wasn't about to let go of him now.

We spoke until three in the morning about what we'd been through in our lives since we had last been together. He was no longer an apprentice editor. In fact, he'd stopped editing altogether. "Too lonely," was how he described it. He had moved on to become an associate producer for a gardening show on cable, and was now a segment producer. Self-deprecatingly, he said he hoped to one day executive produce the gardening show so he could call the shots and finally present the poor weed's point of view.

It was all very easy and I had pangs of guilt for enjoying myself with him; but, as I told him, I'd had so much time to prepare.

There was no turning back with Greg now. I only had one more task that would sadly but finitely break the final link between Jean and me... I had to clean out her house for the realtor to sell it.

This was something I'd been dreading since I'd known Jean wasn't going to make it out of the hospital. And yet, it's something I'd been looking forward to my entire life.

— Chapter Eighteen —

THE COST OF
CLEANING HOUSE

The industrial garbage dumpster was waiting for me when I arrived. I parked at the curb. I wasn't sure at first why I didn't pull into her driveway, but I think it was because all I could imagine was that there were mountains of wood chips still there. "The Ghosts of the Wood Chips," I thought with a chuckle.

It had been some time since I'd stormed from Jean's house and I had not been back since. I gazed from the road at the ramshackle building that I'd grown up in. It seemed so foreign to me; I almost felt as if I was trespassing. It was like that first time returning to high school after graduation. When you're attending the school, it's yours; you own it. But that first time back, you feel as if you just don't belong anymore; that world has moved on without you.

Prepared as I was, I grabbed the box of Hefty Trash Bags (extra-large) that I'd brought, and slowly made my way to the front door. I truly didn't know what to expect, and some sitcom-like scene popped into my head of my hand turning the doorknob only for a sea of items to flow out of the house and carry me away down the street. Perhaps that was more wishful thinking than anything else, since it would have spared me what I estimated to be a month-long operation ahead of me.

There were no lights on in the house as I ever so gently pushed the door open. I don't know why I didn't walk right in, but I guess I expected lots of cobwebs, stale food on the floor, maybe even the odd raccoon or other wildlife nibbling atop mountains of garbage that had taken shape on the floors.

I had mapped out a plan in my head. First I was going to tackle Jean's bedroom. In my mind, since that was the one space she'd had to physically occupy each and every day, that room was the odds-on favorite for finding less junk. I envisioned that placing one large garbage pail in the bathroom would allow me to sweep all toiletries away in one fell swoop. After that I would work my way to my old bedroom, which had turned into a storage facility long ago, and then make my way downstairs to the dining room, den, and kitchen.

Oh, the kitchen! I had this fabulous dream of simply unplugging the refrigerator and wheeling all the discolored food to the curb. Then, upon cleaning out the cupboards of canned foods and bottles, I would set up a stand in the driveway and play "Guess the Expiration Date" with every passerby. Prizes would be whatever money I would find in the cotton balls.

The final two projects, which I considered to be the bulk of the work, would be the basement and the garage. After that I would hire a cleaning crew to scrub and disinfect, then hammer in the "For Sale" sign out front. Ta-da! Done!

Of course, as I entered, there was still that slim optimism in the hard-to-reach places of my mind that Jean might have taken our final blow-up to heart, become introspective, perhaps even seen a psychiatrist and popped a few "make me normal" pills. That faint possibility vanished as soon as the hallway light went on.

There were no intruding carnivores and only a few cobwebs had formed in the corners of the ceilings, so I felt I was off to a good start, but the walls were lined with boxes of cheap gifts she'd picked up at clearance centers; still more boxes of premiums she'd collected over the years with Stanley; and even more boxes of "garage sale collectibles," as she'd sometimes called them. Suddenly, I thought I might relish this day.

I quickly switched on every light in the house, both to give it life and to drive Jean crazy if she was looking down on me. Surely she must have grabbed the wing of some other angel and pointed down to say, "Would you look at my daughter? She thinks she's a billionaire, lighting up the whole city like that." I whipped out my first Hefty trash bag like a gunslinger about to clean up an old west town. I had to show the house I meant business.

I made my way up to Jean's room and my plan quickly fell by the wayside. Her dresser was filled with at least four dozen Avon fragrances and lotions. Some of the bottles were so old, they not only had dust on them, but the sprayers had clogged from dried perfume. Into the trash.

I opened the drawers to the dresser and found every piece of clothing she'd ever owned (no joke, everything!) clumped together. Nothing was folded or laid down nicely. Only one pair of socks gave a hint that any care had been taken; which is why before tossing them, I checked inside. Sure enough, I dipped my hand in and came up with a wad of twenty-dollar bills.

In the closet hung a very small amount of clothes. Jean had wined and dined little. There seemed to be one dress per decade. The sixties were represented by a simple black cocktail dress with the length to hide the knees; the peasant dress was a sure sign of the seventies; the eighties, a unisex pant suit and two pairs of smart slacks, one gray and one black, that were interchangeable with the white and blue blouses I found hanging on the closet door handles.

With the new millennium there had arrived a new look - t-shirts and sweats. Jean had plenty of velvet sweats in dark colors like chocolate brown, charcoal gray, and eggplant purple to match her van. The t-shirts were much more eclectic. She seemed to favor jungle animals more than anything; lions, elephants and giraffes, with the occasional chimpanzee hanging from a vine. Tie-dyes were in high supply, at least twenty or so. I didn't bother counting them as I shoved them into a second hefty bag.

What was astonishing was the collection of free t-shirts she'd managed to acquire at premium shows. In her later years, Jean had become a walking billboard for every business from plumbing suppliers to medical technology companies to fast food and kids' toy manufacturers. Many of these shirts sat in a mountain in the corner of her room. My best guess was that she'd accumulated enough shirts to literally last a lifetime, thereby saving money on water, electricity, and laundry detergent.

My intention was to take these garbage bags of fashion to Goodwill. Something about this donation made me feel as if I was balancing the scales, since, assuming this was where she'd bought the clothes in the first place, Goodwill would be double-dipping.

Once again, the voice from above spoke. "You BUY from Goodwill, C.C.! You SELL at garage sales!" Turning to a neighboring angel… "How did she ever pass her economics class?"

As I heaved the bags over my shoulder, I slid the closet door closed and heard something fall from the back of it. Looking inside, crumpled on the floor was my prom dress.

It was still the same catastrophe that I'd worn, the colors since drained forming a somewhat interesting psychedelic pattern. Jean obviously hadn't washed it, hadn't ironed it, hadn't attempted to fix it. I shook my head, knowing that once again she hadn't had it in her to throw anything away, not even this piece of Cinderelic rag.

The hefty bags went into my trunk and I smacked my hands together, signifying that it was time to get back to work and tackle my old room, aka Storage Locker 5.

The old furniture, a bed, desk and dresser, still remained, and if a forklift could fit in the room, one might actually be able to see them beneath the stacks of full boxes. It probably would have been simpler to just pick up each box and take it out to the curb for the garbage trucks, but the labeling, written in thick black magic marker, sparked some curiosity. One read "Christmas", a second box "C.C. - Birthday", and another "C.C. - Easter".

I opened one Christmas box and found an electric car windshield ice scraper, a "General Hospital" Trivia book, a Rubik's Cube, three matching wine glasses, and a pair of red panties with white fringe that read "Ho-Ho-Ho" on the butt. The items all had one common denominator. They all had "clearance" stickers on them.

I examined each would-be gift more closely. The electric ice scraper had to be plugged in. This meant the car would have needed to be near an outlet, meaning in the garage. Now let's think about this, if the car had been kept in the garage, it wouldn't likely have had much ice on the windshield...

The "General Hospital" Trivia book would have been a fun item, since I'd been a GH junkie in high school and college. Unfortunately the cover was a mistake, though, since all of the questions inside pertained to "All My Children". The Rubik's Cube begged only to ask one question. Why?

The wine glasses were nice enough to use as extras should I run out during some dinner party that I was sure I'd never throw, but I did think three was an odd number to purchase, unless of course they were the only ones left on the shelf. Finally, the most bizarre present that I could have ever received in my entire life, and I was pretty sure for the rest of my living years, were the Ho-Ho-Ho panties. I gave Jean the benefit of the doubt that she hadn't actually gotten the joke of "Ho" smack dab on my ass, and hadn't meant to call me a whore.

The first "Birthday" box was even more informative. First, there was the electric car windshield ice scraper. Yes, there were two, and both were going to be presents for me. Either she'd bought these in bulk, or at a 2-for-1 sale. Next, there was an "I HEART GENERAL HOSPITAL" t-shirt. I was noticing a trend here. Next I pulled out three more wine glasses. So there were a half-dozen after all, I just wasn't meant to get them all at once. I guess she'd been planning on spreading the joy over six months.

Winner of "Best of the Box" was the red bra with white fringe, the matching piece to the "Ho-Ho-Ho" panties. Instead of saying "Ho-Ho-Ho" these said "Hee-Hee-Hee" on each nipple. I realized that since I wasn't getting the bra on Christmas, "Ho-Ho-Ho" wouldn't make much sense at all. Twisted logic, for sure, but Jean's logic just the same.

I burrowed through the rest of the boxes on the lookout for any wads of cash hidden in cotton balls or some other strange form of piggy bank, then carried them down to the dumpster. Greg was going to show up that night to help me take apart the furniture, but I'd promised to have everything gone by then. I looked under the bed and found a few odds and ends, shoe boxes stuffed with trinkets like pens and snow globes and handmade wire bracelets that may have been made by a child at camp, but certainly not by me.

In one Payless shoe box I came across something most unexpected; a car radio. It took no time to recognize it as the one Jean had purchased that awful day at Goodwill. I'd figured that it had ended up in the junkyard with the junk car, but somehow it made it under my bed, perhaps to be my Columbus Day gift.

"That stupid car!" I thought - just another remembrance of an inanimate object that had caused a rift between us. These items, the dress and this radio, had clearly defined the differences between us. I'd always thought to myself that I should be more appreciative, but they were symbols of Jean's weakness, and that was all I could see.

Memory lane did not end there. While cleaning out the garage I came across the sporting equipment she'd secured for our picnic in the park where I'd had my first kiss.

In the laundry room I uncovered every collar for every pet we'd ever owned. Really they had all been handmade from old rope, but each had a cheap tin tag bearing the names: Patches, Petey, Rocky, Leonardo and Candy.

Down in the basement was a treasure trove of Avon products and broken toys. Then, in an old file cabinet, I discovered boxes of old photographs. Sure, there were pictures scattered all over the house, but there was nothing like this one seemingly buried in the deepest recess of the house. It was a sad collection taken during a period Jean had clearly wanted to forget, but like everything else, she'd clung to it. She couldn't let go. They were photos of my mother and father.

There were pictures of them at a lake with a circle of friends; young couples in the beginnings of relationships where you see the future in each other's faces, shaping the looks of future children when two sets of genes would collide. His eyes, her nose, his tone, her color. I could see it in my parents' faces as well.

Jean's smile, her bright, white teeth sparkling in the glare of the sun, told a story of a much better life that had never transpired. That smile. That genuine smile that said, "We are going to have a long and wonderful life together. We are going to raise children together, travel together, grow old together." That was not the life she ended up having. That smile was not one I had seen in my lifetime.

As I think back it seems obvious to me now that she had forced a smile for my sake. Over time, those bright whites had given way to a yellowed dullness that signified someone who didn't care enough about herself to take the same care she'd taken back then. Or perhaps I did live with the real Jean Kurchowski, and she had put on a show for my father that she could never sustain.

As I poured through the rest of the photos, all I could see was me. Someone had to capture the moments, and that was Jean. If only I had thought about it I would have asked for the camera from time to time, but I was too busy acting as if she was putting me out, prodding me to smile. "It's only you and me, kiddo." Except, these pictures only told one side of that story. I was alone in the pictures and it suddenly made me feel alone in the world. She was gone. I suddenly felt the loss, and a tear didn't come to my eye, a stream gushed down my cheeks. I couldn't catch my breath as I sobbed. I suddenly wanted a shoulder, but the only one I needed would never be there for me again.

"This is a joke, right?"

The Cost of Living

I'd fully expected this response when Greg walked in to discover that I'd brought boxes upon boxes of Jean's things back with me. In fact, it looked almost as though I'd picked up Jean's entire hallway and transplanted it in my own. With no photographs, I needed something to hold onto. If asked just a month ago, I sincerely doubt I would have answered that I'd react this way, but reality has a way of switching emotions into actions that one never could have imagined.

To Greg's befuddlement, I highlighted the impact of the items in the boxes - the prom dress and the car radio. I led him into the living room and sat on the seat of a childhood bike I'd found in the garage.

"Do you know what this is?"

He smiled, recognizing it immediately. "It's the bike you were riding the day we met."

It was at that moment when I knew just how much I really meant to him. I had never been religious, and yet I couldn't help but look to the heavens, silently telling my mother, "See? He passed."

"Just tell me you have a plan," he pleaded.

"In the fall, I'll have a garage sale."

FOR MORE INFORMATION

To learn more about M.L. Pressman, ask questions, or

discover what's currently in the works, visit

www.mlpressman.com.